The
Medusa Files

Case 1:
Written in Stone

Gryphon's Gate Publishing

THE DRAGON SPIRIT SERIES
Immortal Coil, Book 1
Shattered Spirits, Book 2

THE MEDUSA FILES

The
Medusa Files

Case 1:
Written in Stone

C.I. BLACK

The Medusa Files, case 1: Written in Stone
Copyright © 2013 C.I. Black

Gryphon's Gate Publishing
550 King St. N.
PO Box 42088 Conestoga
Waterloo, ON.
N2L 6K5

ebook ISBN   978-0-9919229-1-8
Print ISBN   978-0-9937651-1-7

Chapter 1

Every time Morgan closed her eyes she watched the man turn to dust. His face had frozen in terror, his mouth opened in a silent scream, and his skin turned gray and coarse.

Their gazes had locked, and an intense rage had burned across her eyes, setting her face on fire. Cracks had shot through the man's cheeks. They raced to his temples, fracturing into a spider's web.

His hand on her jaw hardened and cracked. One finger broke off, then another. With a snap, his cheek slid free, shattering on the ground beside her head.

She had struggled against his grip, desperate to stop

the inferno in her eyes, desperate to get him off her. But his weight was enormous, his flesh heavy as solid stone.

His wrist cracked, and she shoved him aside. He hit the garbage-strewn asphalt. His head slammed against the dumpster and shattered. Pieces snapped apart, crumbling, until all that remained was dust.

Morgan pressed her palm to her chest where the man's knife had plunged, barely missing her heart. It had been four months. The scar was still raw, and when she closed her eyes and saw him die again, it ached, a burning reminder of the impossible.

She pushed a wild lock of silver hair from her eyes— the bane of her existence ever since she'd realized as a little girl she wasn't supposed to have gray hair and discovered it wouldn't stay dyed.

She dragged her attention across her apartment building's lobby to the dark street outside. Beyond the glass, light reflected in the puddles on the road and sidewalk. At one in the morning, the street was quiet. Her chance of running into anyone was slim. She stepped toward the door. Perhaps it was safe to venture out.

And yet, no matter how many times she told herself it was, she still closed her eyes and watched that man impossibly turn to stone. Even just thinking about him made her eyes burn. She couldn't risk making eye contact and—

God, she couldn't risk that.

When she'd been released from the hospital, she'd

tried to pretend it hadn't happened, that everything was normal.

Except every time she looked someone in the eye, a spark blossomed and the fire threatened to consume her, something that had never happened before that terrible night. She'd locked herself in her apartment, working out relentlessly to keep at bay her fear and frustration, and pacing the too-small rooms like a caged animal.

She was a caged animal. She even went so far as picking up her mail at midnight to avoid meeting anyone and ordering her groceries online, having only the briefest contact with the delivery guy—she could at least avoid looking him in the eye for the thirty seconds it took to answer the door, take the bag, and say thank you.

But no more than that. Every fiber within her being screamed she was dangerous, regardless that she didn't know how or why.

It had happened… It couldn't have happened…

It had to have been the shock of having her head bashed against that dumpster and being stabbed. That was what had made her imagine it and made her imagine the fiery sensation in the days that had followed. She hadn't noticed the burn in at least a month. Maybe it really was her imagination.

Yet she couldn't shake the feeling it had been real and she was dangerous.

Her neighbor stepped into sight, his collar turned up against the April drizzle. He grabbed the handle to the outside door, his gaze meeting hers through the glass. His image wavered. Horns shot from his head, and his nose and jaw morphed into a goat's.

She jerked back.

Her neighbor frowned and opened the door. The image of her attacker turning to stone flashed through Morgan's head, and fire itched around her eyes. She yanked her attention to her mailbox and fumbled with her keys for the smallest one on the ring.

"You're up late, or early." Her neighbor chuckled, a rich sound edged with a hint of nerves. "Or whatever it is."

"Yeah." She bobbed her head, focusing on her keys, trying to blink away the fire. She shouldn't have read that extra chapter in her novel and put herself off schedule. She should have picked up the mail when she usually did. Please just leave. She was dangerous. At the very least, crazy. Just go away.

"Thought you were a ghost. Haven't heard a peep from you since you moved in, what? Four months ago?" He stepped close and slid his key into the lock beside hers. "Did the landlord tell you I work nights and you have to be quiet?"

"No."

He inched closer to reach inside his mailbox, and she fought the urge to shy away. She was not going to be some simpering weakling and fear human contact, although she was still in her yoga sweats and hadn't washed her hair today. In this case, it might be polite to back off.

"I suppose with you up at this hour, you probably work nights as well."

"Unhunh." She didn't work at any time, not since the attack. That, however, was going to have to change soon since her savings were running out. But she just couldn't go back to work, not when reading people and searching their eyes for the truth was such an important part of her job.

Her neighbor locked his box and stepped away—thank God. "Well, see you around."

"See you." She offered a smile, but doubted he saw it, and she wasn't going to look to check if he had. She pressed her forehead against the cool wall of mailbox doors and squeezed her eyes shut. Money was running out, but she was still feeling the fire, and now she was seeing things.

Her attacker crumbling to dust flooded her mind's eye.

She struggled to focus on the lock an inch from her nose. There had to be something she could do that involved working from home. That was best for everyone. Maybe she could be an analyst at the marshal's office, or a researcher, or something.

This was ridiculous. She wasn't dangerous. No one could kill someone with just a look. The sensation of fire was psychosomatic—and she wasn't just psycho.

With a twist, she unlocked her mailbox and pulled out

half a dozen regular-sized envelopes, likely bills, and one large brown envelope. That had to be paperwork from the office. Her boss's not-so-subtle way of telling her it was time to come back to work.

"Deputy Marshal Jacobs?"

She jumped and glanced at the man who'd snuck up on her—not that he'd likely done it on purpose; she just hadn't been paying attention.

His black leather jacket hung open, revealing a black T-shirt straining against a broad well-muscled chest, and his brush-cut dark hair accentuated the chiseled lines of his cheeks and jaw. He raised an eyebrow, drawing her to bottomless brown eyes.

Her pulse pounded, and her breath caught in her throat. She could drown in those eyes, spend an eternity examining their depths and never know all the secrets they kept.

"Deputy Marshal Morgan Jacobs?"

Shit. She'd been staring in his eyes. She jerked her attention to her mailbox. "Who wants to know?"

"The local office said you were here." He leaned against the mailbox doors. His scent enveloped her, a heady mix of musk and mint and all male. She bet his breath was the mint. That made her think of his lips and what they'd feel like under hers. And how terrible she must look with her untamed curls, no makeup, and—

Oh man, she really needed to get out.

She snapped her mailbox closed. "And you just

assumed I was Jacobs?"

"You did open her mailbox." He tapped the apartment number engraved on the door beside her hand.

"Maybe I'm just a helpful neighbor."

"Getting the mail at one in the morning?"

She fought the urge to look at him. She was certain he had a smug smile, and she'd love to wipe it off—or kiss it off—his lips.

Wow, she really did need to get out.

Except going out meant risking that she really was dangerous or crazy or both. She'd hallucinated when she'd looked at her neighbor. What made her think her broken mind wasn't playing tricks on her now with this guy?

"Listen, I also looked at your file. Not a bad picture, I might say."

Wonderful, so the man knew she was on medical leave and likely a nutbar.

"I'd like your consultation on a case."

"I'm not a marshal anymore." It hurt to say it, but it was true, and she was just going to have to live with it. She'd figure something out. She always did.

"This is time sensitive."

"Aren't they always?" She'd been with Fugitive Operations for the United States Marshals Service and almost everything there was time sensitive. The thrill of the hunt was one of the things she'd loved about the job, but she wasn't anything special. There were dozens more marshals like her and there would be dozens more. "I'm sure, Marshal…"

"Gage. Alexander Gage. And it's not marshal."

"I'm sure, *Mr.* Gage, the office can put you in touch with someone more appropriate." She fought the urge to glance at him, or breathe in any more of his heady scent—she wasn't going to ponder how a non-marshal had gotten a look at her file, or what that might mean about who he really was—and turned to the stairs. No way in hell was she waiting for the elevator.

He grabbed her wrist, stopping her. "Please. This is important."

"I'm sorry you've wasted your time." She tugged against his grip, but he held tight.

"If you'd just come with me."

"I don't think so." Who the hell was he to boss her around? She tugged harder. There was no way she was going with him, no matter how much she wanted to step out those doors. She just couldn't risk it. Maybe if he saw she was crazy and dangerous and who-knew-what else, he'd back off.

She lifted her gaze. Just a fraction. But heat flooded her face and eyes, and her pulse raced. What was she doing? She couldn't look at him, couldn't risk being right.

But God, she couldn't be right. That was impossible.

She jerked her attention back to the envelopes now trembling in her hands. Some marshal she was. "I can't help you."

"You don't understand."

She wrenched her arm free. "No, you don't understand. I can't help you." She stepped toward the stairs and the world exploded.

The sound roared over her and the force of the blow shoved her forward, bashing her shins against the first step. Glass and stone flew past, biting her back and legs and arms. Dust filled the air, dancing around her head in the twisting light and shadow.

Ears ringing, she dragged herself around. She reached for the gun at her belt that wasn't there, her brain stuttering, as insanity stepped into the lobby.

A monstrous man towered above Gage. Flecks of rain on his bare chest and arms caught the wildly swinging light above him, accentuating gray, coarse skin.

Behind him, the lobby doors were a wreck of crumpled steel, shattered brick, and shards of glass, as if a truck had plowed through it.

Morgan struggled to breathe. This was not happening. It was impossible. She had to be hallucinating.

But the monster snarled and the muscles in its thick arms bunched. It hefted an enormous hammer and swung at Gage.

Gage ducked. The hammer slammed into the mailboxes with a boom. Metal squealed and bent, and doors flew open.

Morgan ground her teeth. It had to be a normal man. It had to. Her mind was transforming him into a monster—just like the flash of her neighbor moments before. But the vision didn't fade. He whirled toward her, turning inhuman yellow eyes on her, and curled back his lips, revealing large pointy teeth.

Just a man.

"Back off." Gage pointed his gun at the man... monster.

He growled. "That isn't going to stop me."

Gage fired. The man-monster jerked but didn't fall. He swung the hammer toward her.

She threw herself to the side, against the metal railing. The hammer crashed into the stairs beside her.

Another two bangs exploded from Gage's gun. Man-monster roared. Blood oozed from three holes in his chest, but he looked more mad than anything else.

He swung again, and Morgan scrambled back. The hammer crashed into the railing, ripping it from the stairs.

Gage fired another shot.

With a jerk, faster than Morgan thought possible for someone his size, the man-monster tossed his hammer at Gage. It grazed Gage's shoulder, whirling him into the broken mailboxes. His head cracked against a metal door, he sagged, and his gun dropped from his limp hands.

Morgan seized Man-monster's wrist to wrench it around and lock it behind his back, but he twisted and grabbed the front of her shirt. He hauled her up and shoved her into the wall.

Her breath burst from her lungs and her head

slammed against the wall. The man-monster's face wavered. In its place was a normal human face. Square and meaty with a day's worth of stubble on his cheeks and shaved head.

He clasped his other hand around her neck, hefted her, and smashed her into the wall again. She couldn't catch her breath. Her vision blurred and the monster with yellow eyes and fangs leapt back into sight.

She clawed at his hand. It tightened around her neck, and he flashed his fangs at her again. Her lungs burned. Specks danced around her vision. She twisted and kicked him in the groin, drawing a chuckle.

He pressed his enormous weight against her. "Now you're just flirting."

"Fuck you," she said and punched him in the eye.

He staggered back but didn't release his grip. The destroyed lobby twisted in and out of focus.

She swung again, but he jerked back, his arms longer than hers. She dug her nails into his hands, trying to pry his fingers free, but her arms and legs grew heavy, too heavy to fight.

Everything slowed. Her heart, the swinging lamp above them, even the man-monster.

From a great distance away something clicked.

Gage pointed his gun inches from Man-monster's head. Man-monster's eyes widened and the world exploded in a cloud of red mist.

The foyer careened to the side and she hit the floor,

still staring into Man-monster's yellow eyes as blackness swept over her.

Chapter 2

Morgan woke, hurting all over. Her head, her chest, and especially her throat ached. It felt like she'd had one wild night with the girls. Like the time she, Kate, and Izzy had gone to Vegas. Except that had been years ago when they'd all been fresh out of the academy, just before Izzy moved to New York.

She hadn't seen Izzy since. Emailed, yes, but not seen. And Kate, who worked with Morgan at the local marshal's office... well, Morgan didn't know how to explain anything to her—heck, she couldn't even explain it to herself, other than she was crazy—and hadn't talked to Kate since being released from the hospital after the attack. She couldn't even bring herself to email or text her friend. What could she say? She couldn't see her, literally, because she was afraid her gaze would turn her to dust.

What a mess. Morgan drew a deep breath, and sharp pain stabbed across her chest. The memory of the night's events flooded her.

Oh, God.

She *was* crazy. There was no denying it now. Had the man-monster even been real? Her body said his attack had been, but had he been monster or man?

Then the memory of the red mist swept in. Had Gage really blown her attacker's brains out? She struggled to remember, but none of it was clear, only flashes of what had to be hallucination.

She pressed her palms to her eyes, touched something sticky on her cheeks, and peeled them away. Red specks colored her hands. Blood.

Bile burned the back of her throat. He *had* killed that man. Unless the blood was from something else. Please let it have been from something else.

She jerked up and more pain raced across her chest and through her head. The dark room twisted in and out of focus, and she drew quick, shallow breaths, determined to make it settle before she threw up.

Then it hit her. This wasn't her bedroom, and from the king-sized bed, it wasn't a hospital room either—even if the décor was hospital plain.

She tossed back the blanket and scrambled from the

bed. Save for her aching ribs—which didn't feel broken, maybe cracked or bruised—and her sore head and neck, she'd somehow managed to get through whatever had happened unscathed. And thank God she still wore the yoga sweats she'd put on to get the mail that night... morning... she didn't even know what time it was.

Heavy curtains hung to her left, but the light emanating from around the edges was weak. Which could mean it was still very early morning and she hadn't been unconscious for long, or the April rains still darkened the sky—

Or there wasn't a window behind them at all. What if Gage had realized she was crazy and locked her in a psych ward... with fake windows?

That didn't fit with the big bed, but the uncertainty drove her to the window. She yanked the curtains open, sending another spike of pain through her chest, and revealing glass without bars. Rain beaded on the pane, drawing runnels down its clouded surface.

Beyond lay a manicured lawn rolling down to a tall, brick wall. Trees towered above the wall and through the mostly bare branches were the high rises of the city's center. She was still in town. From the look of the wall and the massive trees, in Old Town. Heavy clouds hung in the sky, blotting out the sun, and while she could tell it was day, she had no idea if it was morning or afternoon.

And none of that explained how she'd gotten here or what was going on.

Someone knocked and she eased around to face whoever it was. The door opened with a squeak and light flooded in from a hallway beyond, accentuating Gage's well-muscled form.

She yanked her attention to the floor before her eyes could start burning.

"How are you feeling?" he asked.

"Like I've been hit by a bus."

"An ogre, actually."

"Excuse me?" She couldn't have heard that right.

"Ogre."

Wonderful, now she was suffering auditory hallucinations as well.

Gage shifted, his army boots inching a step into the room. "We really do need to talk, Marshal Jacobs."

"Yes, your urgent matter." She drew in a steadying breath, catching a hint of his scent. Even from across the room he was intoxicating. "I think you've just taken care of that, and I'm not a marshal anymore."

"I said time sensitive, not urgent," he said.

Her gaze darted to him, all sexy muscles and confidence. She dragged it back to the floor. "Fine, time sensitive?"

He shifted again, his feet inching back into the hall. "There are painkillers in the bathroom. Clean up and meet me in the rec room."

"The rec room?"

"To your right. End of the hall." His feet turned to go,

but he didn't walk away. "There's also a pair of sunglasses on the dresser. They might make you feel more comfortable."

And what was that supposed to mean? But before she could ask, he'd shut the door, leaving his intoxicating scent hanging in the room.

She glanced at the dresser. A pair of sunglasses and her mail sat on top. She turned to the only other door in the room. Inside lay a walk-through closet and beyond, the aforementioned bathroom.

Her reflection stared back at her. Even from this distance, at the far end of the closet and in the gray daylight, she looked like the victim of a car crash. Blood streaked across one cheek and stained her sweatshirt and yoga pants around tears in the fabric. She doubted she'd look any better with the light on.

Maybe she could just hide in this room, go back to sleep, and pretend nothing had happened. She was tired enough, sleep might even be possible, but the exhaustion bled into anger. She might have spent the last four months hiding from the world, but not because she was weak and gave up. She wouldn't be weak now.

Except everything had gotten worse. She was seeing things and hearing things. At the very least, she'd been part of… of whatever had happened last night and should be talking with the police. If she was honest with herself, she should go to the closest hospital and get help.

The memory of the man-monster flashed into her

mind. With a jolt, the image jumped to the red mist.

And if she was really honest with herself, she'd pull it together and figure out what the hell was going on. Gage had said he wasn't a marshal, but he'd seen her file.

The key words being 'he'd said'. She had no proof he'd seen it, other than he knew what she looked like and where she lived, and that information could be found through any manner of ways.

She didn't know anything about him, didn't know where she was or what he wanted. She could be in bigger trouble than just fearing to look people in the eye. She had no way of telling what was real and what wasn't. For all she knew, Gage, as she was seeing him, wasn't real either. Which was a shame because he was nice to look at.

She shivered at the thought. That could all just be an extension of her fantasy. How the hell was she going to figure this out? She couldn't even trust herself. How could she trust anyone else?

She'd thought she could get through this herself, but the more she thought about it, the more complicated it became. She'd never know for certain if she wasn't sick. Except she didn't feel sick.

A small part of her whispered this fear, these visions were reality and everything else, what she'd believed was true, was the fantasy. Which didn't make any sense. Monsters didn't exist. And she wasn't one of them.

Which meant she needed to get out of here and get medical help. To do that, she needed to face Gage.

With a flick, she turned on the light and walked through the empty closet into the bathroom, keeping her gaze away from her eyes in the mirror. She'd look everywhere but there. It had been like that since coming home from the hospital. When she did look herself in the eye, what stared back wasn't her. It was alien and strange and gave her the creeps. More evidence there was something wrong with her.

She scrubbed the blood from her face and ran wet hands through her wild curls—doing nothing to tame them. She didn't feel refreshed or better or anything. Just angry and tired and wary.

She grabbed the sunglasses from the dresser and put them on, not wanting to think about how Gage knew they'd make her feel more comfortable. Not that she was going to be looking anyone in the eye anytime soon, but she had to admit, they did feel as if they offered a sense of protection.

It was ridiculous to think pieces of tinted plastic were a defense against anything, but her fear wasn't logical, which meant the solution didn't have to be logical either.

She cracked the bedroom door open and glanced out. Cream walls and a gray carpet—too thick to be institutional—lined the hall. She was at the far end of it, with a small curtained window to her left. To her right were half a dozen doors on either side of the hall. At the end, it looked like two more halls branched off, and straight ahead was an archway opening into a large room, probably the rec room where Gage wanted to meet.

She squared her shoulders, drew in a breath that didn't steady her, and headed down the hall.

"What were you thinking?" a silky masculine voice in the room at the end of the hall asked. "You shouldn't have brought her here."

She froze. Whoever it was, he didn't sound happy.

"And where else was she supposed to go, Lachlin?" That was Gage, his voice softer but edged with steel.

"Any place but here."

She glanced back at the window at the end of the hall. If she exhaled, she might be able to squeeze through. Or better yet, go back to her room and go out that window, except she had no way of knowing if she could get that window open or not.

"You know she won't have a hope of transitioning anywhere else."

Transitioning into what? Crazy? Already there.

"She's not going to be able to transition, period."

"Maybe so. But here is still the only place for her."

Ah, hell no. Whatever was going on, there wasn't an *only* anything, and they weren't going to force her.

She inched closer. Maybe if she could get to the intersecting hall she'd be able to escape without anyone noticing.

"We're short a member. In time—"

Silky Voice, Lachlin, snorted. "Time can't help her."

Only a few more feet to the intersection, but now she

could see into the room. It was indeed a rec room with two sofas and three comfy chairs huddled around a big screen TV, a pool table beside them, and a full wall lined with books and board games.

Gage stood with his back to her in front of the pool table, his arms crossed. On the other side by the sofas stood a tall man—taller than Gage—but narrower all over. He was lithe grace if Gage was solid muscle. Black hair hung loose around his shoulders… or was that down his back? She couldn't tell, and the moment she thought she could, it seemed to change. His narrow face was breathtakingly beautiful. It tugged at something within her, drawing her to him, yearning to bask in such perfection.

She ground her teeth against the desire and pressed against the wall, praying he wouldn't notice her.

"Regardless," Gage said, "we still need to bring her up to speed."

"There's no bringing her up to anything. She's a changeling and a half-breed at that. You can't fix that." Lachlin dropped onto the sofa, making something so simple look smooth and sexy and inviting. "We all want Chava back, but this girl isn't the answer."

A huge shadow emerged from the hall to her right and stepped into the entranceway to the rec room. The man was enormous, as tall as Lachlin but at least three times the width. He was muscles upon muscles like the man-monster who'd attacked her last night. Except instead of gray skin covered in coarse hair, he was smooth, rich ebony.

"I don't want to replace Chava either," the large man said, his voice a deep rumble.

"See, even Clayton is smart enough to know this is a bad idea." Lachlin grabbed the remote and turned on the TV.

Gage flicked a finger and the TV snapped off. "She's got skills for the job."

She did not just see that. Did she?

"I hate when you do that." Lachlin turned the TV back on. "But if she can't see through glamour, she's useless. The odds of a changeling breaking the psychological compulsion not to see us are impossible."

"Those aren't odds," Clayton said.

Lachlin glared at him. "And even if she can, she's a half-breed. She'll go mad first."

She already was mad. Their words whirled through her. They didn't make any sense and yet a small part of her felt maybe if she concentrated hard enough, she'd figure it out.

"The boys really do natter," said a soft, feminine voice beside Morgan.

She jumped and bit back a yelp. There, at her elbow, stood a tiny woman of East Indian descent with bright purple hair, the short locks spiked in all directions.

Her features were delicate, a match to her less than five-foot-high petite frame. Her chin, nose, and ears extended into points, wavered, then blunted back to normal human features, then extended again. For a heartbeat her eyes were purple, like her hair, then back to dark brown.

"I'm Rika. It's good to have another girl in the house again."

The large black man turned, his eyes wide, his mouth in a silent 'oh'.

"Don't just stand in the hall, Clayton," Lachlin said. "Bring the girl here."

Morgan rolled her eyes. As if he was so much older than her. In fact, he looked younger, mid-twenties to her early thirties. "I'm hardly a girl."

"Trust me, Kitten, to me you're practically a babe in arms." His ears morphed like Rika's into long, delicate points then jumped back to normal. He turned to Gage. "You see why she can't be here."

"You're only worried she's Kin enough to see through your charm." Rika ushered Clayton into the room, making space for Morgan.

Lachlin rolled his eyes. "She's half-human. That isn't Kin at all."

"It's Kin enough for your sister," Clayton said.

Lachlin shot upright. "We are not talking about my sister."

"No, we're not. We're talking about Chava's daughter, half-human and changeling or not." Gage turned to Morgan and extended his hand.

She stared at it. She didn't want to take it. She had no idea what they were talking about, but without a doubt they were crazier than she was. At least she knew she'd lost it. Unless, of course, she wasn't hearing the conversation right. "I think I'm with Lachlin. I don't belong here."

"That's because you don't understand." Gage inched his hand closer.

Her gaze leapt to his bottomless brown eyes. Through the sunglasses, they seemed darker and deeper than before. She could drown in those eyes and be happy.

And she could kill him with a look.

She jerked her attention back to the floor.

"Ah, shit." Lachlin slammed the remote on the coffee table. "She knows."

"Argue with that." Rika grabbed Morgan's hand and squeezed.

"She's going to kill us before our job does," Lachlin said.

Morgan pulled her hand free from Rika's. "Knows about what? What the hell are you talking about?"

"It's what we need to discuss. Why don't we find someplace more private," Gage said.

She didn't want to be alone in a room with him… okay, well, maybe she did, but at least she was smart enough to know right now that was a bad idea. "How about the hall."

Gage's eyes narrowed, but he stepped into the hall and

slightly around the corner.

Morgan followed, keeping the rec room and the others in sight. "So?"

She wanted to look at him, stare him straight in the eye, and read him like she used to read suspects and sources when chasing fugitives. But she couldn't risk it. Not with that voice in her head getting louder and louder, saying she was dangerous.

Gage shifted and twisted a silver ring on his right index finger. "From the way you averted your eyes, you already know your gaze is dangerous, and I suspect you're now seeing things."

"We'll assume that's true." She didn't want to give him any proof she was crazy or that she bought into his craziness.

He arched an eyebrow. "You have a terrible poker face."

She could just punch him. "Fine. Your friend, Lachlin, mentioned a changeling. That's a fairy child replacing a human child."

"Very good."

"Don't get cocky." Even if that confidence completely turned her on. "I took first year mythology as an elective in college."

"Not sure that will help." He shifted again, drawing her back to his eyes. "You know within you something is different. You know the world around you is different from what you were told and you think you're losing your mind."

She pulled her gaze to the wall behind his right ear. "Oh, and that's because I'm a changeling like Lachlin says. That would mean I'm a fairy who grew up in the human world." She'd known from a young age she was adopted, but a changeling? That was ridiculous.

Except the part of herself that knew the heat in her eyes wasn't her imagination told her what Gage said was true. But that just meant she really was crazy.

"Not quite a fairy but one of the Kin."

"Kin?"

"Yes. Everything likely mentioned in that mythology course you took and more."

"This is a joke, right?" Maybe she wasn't crazy. Maybe Izzy had told Kate that Morgan was moping and they'd plotted something outrageous to brighten her up. It wasn't likely, but Izzy could have convinced Kate drastic measures were necessary.

"This isn't a joke, Kitten," Lachlin called from the rec room, miming his head exploding.

Gage glared at him then turned back to Morgan. "When you look at Lachlin, what do you see?"

One hot, arrogant guy. "What do you mean?"

"You see two Lachlins, don't you. You see a human face and a face that's more than human. He's fae. Just like when you looked at the ogre, you saw his human glamour as well as his real appearance. Kin can see other Kin."

"So why couldn't I *see* any of this before?" Still not

going to buy it, but she couldn't help asking. Besides, she couldn't be Kin. She wasn't some kind of mythological monster.

"It's complicated."

"Well, make it uncomplicated or I'm out of here." And really, she should have gone a long time ago, but she couldn't make herself leave. It was like watching a car accident. That was it. She was watching herself go crazy and couldn't bring herself to look away.

Gage twisted his ring again. "Sometimes half-humans, like you, are left to be raised by humans because the chance of them having enough Kin blood to be Kin is slim. Hence they become changelings. Kin abilities show up around puberty, and when you didn't manifest your abilities, your mother probably thought you were too human and it was better to leave you alone. Non-Kin can't see through glamour."

"But Kin can."

"Yes, and because you've recently come into your power, you're starting to see past the glamour."

"And every Kin has this glamour?" Did that mean she had a glamour? Was that what she was seeing through when she looked in the mirror and a stranger stared back?

"Yes. Everything magical does. It's a type of universal magic that keeps magic protected and hidden from humans." Gage crossed his arms. "Humans can't usually see through glamour and with the current belief that the Kin don't exist, it's almost impossible to get them to see through it. If they do, the glamour will change their memories, so they can't remember what they've seen."

"So you're telling me there are monsters walking around, looking like humans?" And that she was one of them, or rather half of one.

He raised an eyebrow. "You worked for Fugitive Operations. You don't have to be Kin to be a monster."

He had a point. But her head still whirled. She didn't want to accept it, and she had no proof any of it was real. It was just so hard to remember she couldn't trust her judgment.

"And you're telling me I'm one of those monsters?"

"Here it comes," Lachlin said.

Gage's expression darkened. "One more word and I swear—"

Lachlin jerked up and leaned over the back of the sofa, sneering. "You'll what?"

The lights in the room flickered and dimmed. Clayton's eyes widened and Rika hugged herself. The air crackled with pent-up energy and the hair on Morgan's arms and neck stood up.

"You can't do anything," Lachlin said.

"Try me," Gage growled. The lights flared bright and returned to normal.

Lachlin snorted and slumped back down on the couch.

To hell with this. She was getting out of this crazy house. She couldn't believe anything Gage said, and she certainly couldn't believe she was some kind of monster.

A bright chime rang and Rika pulled a glittery purple phone from her back pocket. "Yeah?"

Gage held out his hand to Morgan. Light flashed from the ring on his finger. "I know this is a lot to take in, but it's important you understand it."

"Police report a break-in at 23 Park Street," Rika said.

Lachlin changed the channel. "Because our mighty leader was just there."

Rika tapped her foot. "Beyond the car driving through the front doors."

"A car drove through the front doors? I thought—?" But Morgan wasn't sure what she thought. She was a monster. No, damn it. That wasn't true.

"I had to say something to explain the destroyed lobby," Gage said.

"And the ogre didn't get anywhere near the fifth floor," Rika said.

"The fifth floor?" That was her floor.

Rika pocketed her phone. "Apartment 522."

Gage reached for Morgan but hesitated and didn't grab her arm. Even Lachlin straightened.

"That's—" She didn't know if she wanted to scream or sob.

"Your place," Clayton said.

"What have you gotten me involved in?" It was bad enough she didn't even know if she'd been attacked or not, but now her apartment, her private space, had been violated.

"That's complicated," Gage said.

"More complicated than Kin and changelings and fairies?"

Lachlin snickered and Rika glared at him.

"That's it. I have to go." She couldn't stand there any longer. She had to get back to her apartment.

Gage grabbed her arm. "You're not going anywhere."

"She's a snake charmer. She's hardly helpless," Lachlin said.

Gage turned on him, his grip iron around her arm. "It's too dangerous. Not until we know what's going on."

And boy, would she love to know what was going on, but not until she'd seen the damage to her place. Those rooms, the locked front door, were the only things that were real to her. She was not going to lose that, too—that and it made an excellent excuse to get the hell out of there.

She seized Gage's hand, wrenched her arm around— breaking free of his grasp—and yanked his hand around to his back, holding him close. His scent slid around her, captivating her senses, and she ground her teeth against its charm.

"Planning to keep a U.S. marshal captive isn't viewed well by the rest of law enforcement."

Gage chuckled, the deep sound vibrating through his back into her chest. "I thought you weren't a marshal anymore."

"I'm leaving."

"Told you. Changelings just can't take it." Lachlin leaned back and switched channels again.

"Not helping," Gage said, but nothing about him indicated he was worried about her.

Lachlin shrugged. "You said you wanted her on the team, but in a few minutes it'll really sink in and Clayton will have to mop her brains off the floor."

"I'm fine and I'm leaving." They could easily stop her. Four to one odds were terrible even if she'd had her gun.

Gage drew in a breath, his chest expanding, pressing his warm back against her. "Why don't I explain more after we assess the damage to your apartment?"

"Excuse me?" Her mind stuttered over that. It didn't make sense for him to just give up, unless of course he really did want her cooperation. He'd said he'd wanted her to join some team. Holding her prisoner wasn't really a good start to any partnership.

"Can you please let me go?" But she wasn't sure from his tone if he wanted her to let him go or not. Or were those her feelings? Ah, shit.

"Fine." But there still wasn't any way to tell what was real and what wasn't. She didn't know what was worse, losing her mind or knowing it was happening. And none of that mattered until she found out what had happened to her apartment.

Chapter 3

She drove with Gage and Lachlin to her apartment building while Rika and Clayton stayed at the house, which indeed had been a small estate in Old Town.

No one said a word during the five-minute drive.

Gage parked his black Mustang between two police cars. Their flashing lights painted the ruined front of Morgan's apartment building in red and blue strobes and sparkled in the puddles. It did look as if a car had crashed through the double doors into the staircase, and sure enough, a tow truck was loading a mangled midsized car onto its flatbed. But she couldn't shake the memory of the man-monster... the ogre—according to Gage—

attacking her.

She still didn't know how she felt about what they'd told her regarding changelings and fairies, or rather the Kin—whatever they were.

"What happened to the body?" she asked.

Gage glanced at her through the rearview mirror, his expression clear he didn't want to answer her. "We have a specialist who adjusted his injuries to match the accident."

"And by specialist, you mean...?" She wasn't sure she wanted the answer and she didn't know if she believed him.

"Let's see if this will be what breaks the changeling's mind." Lachlin chuckled and got out of the car.

Gage glared at him. "Think of this specialist like a cross between an undertaker and a pathologist."

"Sure." Whatever that meant. It all seemed impossible. Hell, everything she knew about the world said it was impossible.

Except the tiny part of her that said she was dangerous believed Gage. But without hard proof—which she wasn't even sure she'd believe given she doubted her sanity—she had to err on the side of reality. Yes. She had to be practical.

But that voice inside her was getting harder and harder to deny.

She got out with Gage and they joined Lachlin at the building's front door. A work crew was already fixing the mess of her lobby, clearing away rubble and twisted steel, while a police officer stood on the curb watching it all.

Morgan followed Gage and Lachlin to the elevator at the end of the hall—since the stairs were roped off—and Lachlin pressed the call button. He hadn't given her a second look since leaving the house. The air around him was practically frigid. And yet there was something that drew her to him. Perhaps the hint of lithe grace, or his chiseled features. It couldn't be his arrogance, which was impossible to ignore, even beyond the model-hot looks. Sure, some girls liked bad boys, but Morgan had spent more than enough time arresting them to know they were just trouble.

Gage shifted beside her. He was a completely different story from Lachlin. Rugged, masculine, tough. He exuded confidence and a hint of violence like a well-honed soldier. She'd bet he'd spent time in the army, probably special forces or the marines. And his scent. God, just standing beside him was driving her crazy... all right, more crazy.

The elevator doors opened and her heart skipped a beat at the thought of being in close quarters with either of the men.

She shoved the thought aside and entered. Gage and Lachlin followed, drawing a shiver she fought to hide. Her thoughts were just because of the shock of everything that had happened—and the months of being locked in her apartment... the apartment that had been ransacked.

The bell dinged and the doors opened. Halfway down the hall, her apartment door stood open. A well-muscled male uniformed officer stood in the entrance flirting with a female forensic tech, while a man in a gray suit—his back to her—talked with her neighbor.

Her throat tightened at the invasion of her sanctuary.

She sucked in a steadying breath, surprised at how intense the feeling was. This was their job. She'd done it herself and it didn't mean anything. But that apartment had been her safe house. She just hadn't realized how dependent she'd become on it.

"Hey." Her neighbor waved at her and the man before him turned around.

"Oh, great," Lachlin mumbled. "Wright."

The man, a middle-aged guy with salt-and-pepper hair cut short around a bald spot, tapped a pen to his notepad and headed her way. He looked familiar. She must have seen him the last time she'd visited the local police department, but she hadn't had any dealings with him.

Gage reached into his leather jacket and pulled out his identification. "Special Agent Alexander Gage."

So he was FBI. Did that make him more or less trustworthy?

"I remember you, Special Agent. Detective Wright." The muscle in Wright's jaw twitched. Guess it wasn't a positive memory. He turned to her. "Morgan Jacobs?"

Over Wright's shoulder, her neighbor's eyes widened

in shock, but she couldn't tell at what. He didn't seem to
be looking at her but at Lachlin or maybe Gage. Her
neighbor's face morphed into the goat's then back to
human, and she bit the inside of her cheek. Don't react.
Don't let the detective know she was crazy. "Yes."

"And you just so happened to show up with the FBI?"

Lachlin shrugged. "Job interview."

Wright tapped his pen on his pad. "At seven in the
morning?"

"Is Marshal Jacobs a suspect in the break-in of her
own apartment?" Gage asked.

Wright held Gage's dark stare.

Gage raised an eyebrow and Lachlin rolled his eyes.
Wonderful, it looked like this was going to turn into a
pissing contest.

She stepped ahead of Gage, drawing Wright's
attention. She adjusted her gaze to the empty air just
beside his head and prayed the sunglasses hid the fact she
wasn't making eye contact. "Let's just fast-track to the
part where you let me evaluate the damages."

"Not sure you really want to," Wright said, but he
stepped aside anyway, giving her a clear view through the
door.

Her stomach lurched. It was destroyed. Her apartment
had been violated beyond recognition. Her furniture was
torn apart, tables and chairs smashed, everything hanging
on the walls had been ripped down save for one painting
which hung at a precarious angle, and stuffing from her

couch and comfy chair littered the debris like fake Christmas snow gone wild.

"Anything missing?" Wright asked. At least he sounded contrite at such a ridiculous question.

Nothing and everything could be missing. She had no idea how she was going to be able to tell. Her television had been knocked over but hadn't been taken. The hutch with her grandmother's china and silver had been toppled to the floor as well, but if they'd taken anything, she couldn't tell since silver and pieces of china littered the floor around it.

"Do you see anything?" Gage asked.

"Well, they weren't after valuables." She picked her way through the mess to her desk. Her laptop hung behind it, caught on its power cord and the cord for her printer—which lay on its side a few feet away.

"Not your usual burglary," Wright said.

"No. Might have something to do with work." Maybe someone she'd apprehended had found out where she lived and wanted payback. But finding that out meant she'd have to talk to Kate, and that would make their initial conversation since the attack even more awkward. 'I'm not calling because I miss you, but because of work.' Oh yeah, she was a great friend.

"I'll follow up with the work lead. You're a U.S. Marshal?"

She nodded.

"Even if it is work, unless they left prints or we get

lucky with something else, the odds aren't good we'll catch anyone. Particularly if they're not trying to pawn anything you can identify."

"Thank you, Detective. I'll have Jacobs contact you if she thinks of anything." Gage ushered Wright to the door, shook the man's hand, and watched him go. Her neighbor continued to peer in from the far side of the hall. Gage shot him a hard look and her neighbor scurried off.

In that moment, there was something dark and powerful about Gage. Morgan still had no idea if she could trust him, and for a heartbeat she didn't care. For that heartbeat, she wanted the intensity of that stare on her and the power it promised wrapped around her and within her. Without a doubt, that intensity translated to the bedroom. She knew it the same way she knew she was dangerous. And she wanted him. Craved him.

Holy shit. She really had lost her mind.

Gage closed the door and turned to face her. Warmth swept over her cheeks. This was so embarrassing.

Lachlin blew out a sigh. "All right, fine. You were right."

Ice consumed the warmth. "Right about what, specifically?"

"But that doesn't mean she can completely accept the reality about Kin." Lachlin picked at a piece of fluff from the broken back of her couch. "I'm pretty sure she still doesn't understand what you told her at the house. She certainly didn't believe you."

"Right about what?" She wanted to stare at Gage, give him the same hard look he'd given her neighbor, but everything within her said that was a bad idea— particularly if she wanted him flesh and blood and in her bed. She crossed her arms instead.

"Remember I said that matter I wanted to discuss with you was time sensitive."

"You would have been better off being more direct and saying someone wanted to trash my apartment."

"More like someone wants you dead."

"Yep, that would have gotten my attention better than asking about a case and saying it was a time-sensitive matter," she said.

Lachlin snorted. "You actually said it was time sensitive?"

Gage picked his way into the room toward her. "I didn't want to frighten you."

Good God! Men. "You know I apprehend criminals for a living." She wasn't some damsel in distress. She wasn't even that feminine, never had been, and what with all the working out she'd been doing in the last four months, she had even less girlish curves than before.

"And an ogre tried to rip her head off," Lachlin said. "I'm sure she suspected something was up."

"Yeah." She wasn't going to add that she still wasn't sure she believed that… no matter how right it felt. As soon as she was alone in a hotel room, she was calling

Izzy and finding out just who Alexander Gage, FBI, really was.

She reached over her desk to grab her laptop. Something silver and shiny caught her eye, poking out from beneath a pile of scattered papers and pens on her desk. It looked like a cell phone, except hers was black.

"What is it?" Gage asked.

He must have seen her hesitate. Even Lachlin leaned forward, his air of indifference gone. He noticed her attention and leaned back, the indifference returning.

Interesting, there was more to Lachlin than met the eye. Of course, there was more to Gage and everyone else she'd met in that house, she was certain of that.

She grabbed a pencil and pushed the papers aside, revealing a silver phone. The touch screen lit up, and a red message alert flashed, indicating one message. "I think, according to our local detective, we might just have gotten lucky."

She pressed the pencil's eraser end to the message alert. The phone chimed, the screen went black, then brightened into a photo. Center on the screen was her friend Kate, gagged and bound to a chair.

Morgan's heart skipped a beat. "Oh, God."

Blood crusted Kate's right temple and her right eye was swollen shut. Her expression was hard and angry. If she got free, hell would have no fury compared to what she'd do to her captors. At the bottom of the picture were two words: We'll call.

Chapter 4

Morgan stared at the picture of her friend bound and bleeding. She couldn't stop looking at it.

Gage swore under his breath. "We can handle this."

"You're not handling anything. A marshal has been abducted. This is a matter for the marshals and the police." If, in fact, Kate had been abducted. Morgan was jumping to conclusions. A panicked reaction at seeing the photo, at the whole damned morning. She needed to do what she'd been trained to do, and that meant keeping her cool.

"Except the message was obviously left for you. That makes it our business," Gage said.

But she knew he didn't mean FBI business. "You mean because I'm Kin."

"Why do you think they didn't ask for a ransom?"

"I'm sure they'll get around to it."

"Why would they even ask you for one? If you had a fortune, you wouldn't be living here." Gage gestured to her ruined living room.

And that was what bothered her. Why her? And why Kate? It had to have something to do with their job as marshals.

"If the kidnappers do ask for a ransom, it'll be a lie. They're after you," Gage said.

"Don't be ridiculous." But even as she said it, the words sounded false.

"Even I can't believe your luck is so bad as to be attacked, have your apartment ransacked, and your friend kidnapped all in the same morning," Lachlin said.

"I would bet whoever's responsible is Kin. The marshal's office isn't qualified to deal with them. You want your friend back alive, you stand back and let me deal with this."

"No." This was her friend and she sure as hell didn't trust Gage, no matter how good he smelled.

Gage raised an eyebrow. "I'm not sure you have much of a say in the matter."

"I'm not some helpless damsel in distress."

"Six hours ago you had no idea Kin even existed. You're not ready for this," he said.

"Try and stop me."

Lachlin snickered. "Go on, Gage. Stop the snake charmer."

Morgan glared at him. "Stop saying that." Heat raced across her eyes and gray swept over the picture precariously hanging behind him. It cracked and fell, shattering on the floor.

Lachlin jerked away. "I told you she was dangerous."

The heat swelled, racing over her face. The edge of her toppled chair in front of Lachlin hardened.

"Morgan," Gage said, panic edging his voice.

"Stop looking at me!" Lachlin's face morphed back and forth between normal and Kin. "Stop looking."

"Close your eyes," Gage said.

Her eyes were on fire. A gray haze filled her vision.

"For God's sake, close your eyes."

The chair crumbled. Lachlin drew his sidearm. Gage grabbed for it, but Lachlin twisted out of the way. The wall behind them cracked. Oh, God.

"Close your eyes," Gage yelled.

She wrenched her gaze to the floor. The inferno raged over her cheeks and forehead. Stop, please. Just stop. She squeezed her eyes shut. Pressure pounded against her lids. She pressed her palms to her eyes. She was going to explode. It was too much. She was burning alive. She couldn't control it. She really was crazy.

And she was dangerous.

Something brushed her shoulder. It settled on her

forearm, a hand, sure and strong. Musk and mint slid across her senses. Gage.

"That's it. Focus. Take a deep breath." His voice eased over her, cutting through the roaring in her head, a cool balm on a sunburn.

She drew in a ragged breath. The pressure pulsed in her eyes.

"Another breath."

The heat billowed but not as ferocious as before. She sucked in another breath. Her pulse slowed and the pressure eased even more.

"Lord and Lady," Lachlin said. "Through the damned sunglasses even."

The heat threatened to roar over her again. She forced in another breath.

Gage squeezed her arm. "That's it. Just focus on being calm."

"Calm?" The word came out edged with hysteria. "I turned my chair to stone." And her painting and wall and that man who'd attacked her. Stone!

Gage's other hand rubbed a gentle circle between her shoulder blades. "I know."

"To stone."

"It happens."

"It doesn't just happen. It can't happen." Gage had said the Kin were every monster mentioned in her mythology class, and the most famous one who turned people to stone was Medusa, one of three gorgon sisters.

Her stomach lurched. "I can't be."

"Morgan," Gage said, his voice soft.

"How can I?" Her gaze leapt up to the chaos and the crumbled stone that she'd made.

Lachlin winced, but Gage met her gaze as if he could hold her essence, shelter it from the storm inside her with just a look.

"Gorgons aren't real. I can't be— My reflection—"

"The mythology books don't usually have all the details right."

"Obviously, since looking at your reflection won't turn you to stone," Lachlin said.

The muscle in Gage's jaw twitched. "Gorgon is a race. A very rare race, and the ability is only passed through the female line."

"But what does that mean?" She didn't want to know. And yet she'd just proven how dangerous she was. If she didn't want to kill someone else, she had to know. "And what about the sunglasses? Why didn't they turn to stone?"

"It's all about focus," Gage said. "Your gaze turns what you look at to stone. You're looking through the sunglasses, hence your power goes right through them."

"Except the tint in the glass and the fact they're so close to your face is supposed to trick your powers into thinking something is in front of your eyes and hold your powers back." Lachlin shifted, his indifference looking forced. "Obviously you're an exception to the rule."

"Let's get you back to the house, and I'll explain everything," Gage said.

She nodded, forcing her gaze down. Kate stared back at her from the phone forgotten in her hand. She couldn't go anywhere. She had to pull it together. "No. Kate is the priority."

"And Lachlin and I will find her," Gage said.

"No. I won't just sit around and wait." She hadn't hurt anyone since leaving the hospital, and just a few minutes ago, the hall outside her apartment had been filled with people and she hadn't gone all eye crazy on them. Lachlin had pissed her off. The man in the alley had scared her and pissed her off. She couldn't believe she was even thinking about this. "My temper is the trigger. I keep it in check, furniture stays normal."

"You can't just roam the streets," Lachlin said.

"Stop telling me what I can and cannot do." Heat flickered around her eyes. Furious, she ground her teeth and forced it back. "Kate is the priority. I can control this."

And she wasn't going to think about how the impossible had suddenly become terrifying reality. Kin were real. She was a monster. And none of that mattered. She needed to figure out if Kate really had been abducted and, if so, rescue her.

'The Imperial March' from *Star Wars* sounded, weak and tinny.

"What the hell is that?" Lachlin asked.

"My phone. My boss is calling." She scanned the floor around her. She'd left the phone on her desk when she'd gone to get her mail. It had to be somewhere in the mess.

The tune chirped again. To her left? Under the shredded cushion?

Gage shoved aside the couch. Not under there. She tossed the cushion over it and gathered the papers underneath, blowing off bits of fluff.

Another chirp. There, a hint of light from the phone's face under a book.

She grabbed it and turned it on. "Jacobs."

"You all right?" her boss, Supervisory Deputy U.S. Marshal Ed Waters, asked. "I just got word about your apartment." His gruff voice was even more gruff than usual, which meant he'd been worried... or it had been too long since she'd heard it and she wasn't used to it anymore.

"I'm fine. I was out when it happened. Looks like—"

"Don't get him involved," Gage hissed.

She glared at him, realized what she was doing, and jerked her attention back to the floor.

"Looks like what?" Ed asked.

"Like complete chaos. The police are on it. I'm sure they'll do their job."

"I'm sure." Ed's tone darkened even more. Yeah, she didn't like the idea of letting someone else handle any of this either, but marshals didn't deal with break-and-enters. "You got a place to stay for a while? And don't tell me you're staying there. We don't know if this is case related or not."

She bit back a snort. She was pretty sure it wasn't case related. "Fine. Is Kate there? I'll stay with her."

Gage's feet shifted closer. "What are you doing?"

"She called in sick this morning," Ed said. "Well, actually, emailed. It was pretty early when she sent it."

Shit. So the photo on the phone could be true. "I'll try her at home."

"You call if you need anything."

"I will."

"And Jacobs…"

"Yeah, Boss?"

"You better be coming back."

That was the closest she was going to get to him confessing he missed her, and she had no idea how to respond to that. "I gotta go."

"Unhunh."

The line went dead and she turned to Gage, keeping her gaze just past his shoulder. "Kate emailed in sick early this morning."

"Is there any doubt the photo is real?" Lachlin asked, his casual arrogance returning.

"I don't believe everything I see. And maybe she is just sick. I'm going to her house to find out." She pocketed both phones and picked her way to her door.

"You can't just let her roam the streets," Lachlin said.

"We've already proven you can't stop me." And she

sure as hell wasn't going to sit back and let these strangers look for Kate, FBI, Kin, or whatever the hell they were.

Chapter 5

Kate's house only confirmed she'd been abducted. The front door had been left unlocked, the key table in the foyer knocked over, and her cell phone smashed into pieces beside it, giving evidence of a struggle. Aside from that, however, there was no indication who was responsible or where Kate might be.

They returned to the estate in Old Town to a room Gage called the situation room. Rika took the kidnapper's phone, transferred everything on it to a computer set into the large table in the middle of the room, and handed the phone back. Then she perched on a stool at the far end and tapped on the table's surface.

The picture of Kate appeared on the big screen monitor at the back of the room, blown up to ridiculous proportions. Everything but Kate was dark, and there were only hints of a cinderblock wall behind her. There wasn't even a window in the shot. The blood on Kate's temple had caked to her skin in a thick line to her jaw, pasting a lock of blonde hair to it, so she'd been upright when it had dried, which only proved if she'd been unconscious it hadn't been for long.

Rika pursed her lips. Her ears turned pointed and her features more delicate, and stayed that way. She rolled a purple spike of hair between her fingers and stared at the screen embedded in the table.

Clayton sat on the stool beside her, his dark, hulking presence becoming unnaturally still. Morgan didn't know anyone who focused to the point where it looked as if he didn't breathe.

"This is going to take a while," Rika said without looking up. "I'll run an algorithm that'll hopefully extract more detail, but until it's done, it's normal eyes at work."

"I'll see what I can find," Clayton said, his deep voice a soft rumble.

"Good. There's got to be something there." Gage draped his leather coat on the back of a chair, leaned over the table, and examined the computer screen embedded in it.

Lachlin strolled in with a mug, steam curling over the lip. "So what's the plan?"

The rich aroma of coffee wafted over Morgan's senses and her stomach growled. She hadn't had anything to eat since dinner last night. Funny how she'd thought to get her sidearm from the gun safe in her bedroom but hadn't thought to grab anything to eat. Guess she now knew what her priorities were.

Gage tapped on the table and swiped across it. The picture of the man-monster took Kate's place, along with his rap sheet. "We have an I.D. Daryl Matas. Assault, possession, and possible gang ties."

"And we still don't know if the attack on me is related to Kate's abduction," Morgan said.

"It's too much of a coincidence not to be." Gage crossed his arms, straining his T-shirt across his broad shoulders and around his biceps. "We have to assume the goal of the abduction is to get another chance at you and we have to assume, because Matas was involved, it's Kin related."

"And we have to assume they want you dead." Lachlin hooked a waist-length strand of black hair behind a pointed ear.

"But why would any Kin want me dead? I didn't even know they... you existed a few hours ago."

"Gorgons are rare and extremely powerful," Gage said.

Lachlin snorted and took a sip from his coffee.

"Some Kin react badly to that kind of power and see you as a threat. Because you've come into your power, anyone who sees you will know you're a gorgon." Gage wasn't saying something. It was subtle in his tone and how the others glanced at him—save for Clayton who didn't move—before they turned back to their work, or in Lachlin's case, his coffee. Maybe everyone was waiting to see if she'd lose it and turn them all to stone.

"So sometime in the last four months I've run into someone who recognized what—" God, she didn't want to say it. "—what I am?"

"Exactly. I know it's tough, but there has to be someone. They probably acted surprised when they saw you," Gage said.

It wasn't going to be tough. She hadn't communicated with a lot of people in the last four months, and she'd looked at them even less when talking with them, although in the hospital— "There were tons of people in the hospital after I…"

"Used your power," Lachlin said.

"Yes." The image of her attacker crumbling to dust flashed into her mind and a hint of fire licked at her face. She slid her gaze to the wall beside the big screen and forced the fire back.

"It would have taken at least a few weeks for your power to fully manifest," Gage said.

Power she didn't want.

"After that, you'd be recognized as Kin," Lachlin said.

Well, that narrowed it down. She hadn't spent long in the hospital and she'd only ventured outside in the week after. The fear that she was dangerous had been so overwhelming, she'd found her new apartment and cut ties with everyone who knew her even on a casual basis, including her best friends, her job, and her parents. She'd sequestered herself, determined to keep everyone safe until she'd figured out what was going on. "There hasn't been anyone."

"Well, there has to be someone." Lachlin set his cup on the table and Rika picked it up, glaring at him with bright purple eyes.

God, Morgan was never going to get used to that.

"What about your neighbor?" Gage asked. "He recognized you."

"We'd just met last night. Just before you showed up."

"Not enough time for him to call someone and have them send Matas after you," Rika said, extending the cup closer to Lachlin.

"Maybe enough time for a kidnapping." Lachlin took the cup back. "Perhaps they are two separate incidents."

"No, it feels more like your friend's abduction was a result of Matas's failure," Gage said. "We need to figure out who saw past your glamour."

Lachlin rolled his eyes. "Anyone could have seen past her glamour. It's completely blown apart."

"Glamour works on Kin as well? I thought it just worked on humans."

"If you've got control of it, most Kin won't be able to see past it," Gage said. Which made her wonder if what she saw was really him or his glamour.

"Unless you're one of a few *special* Kin who can see past almost anything," Lachlin said, his tone clear he was not one of the special Kin. "Like a gorgon."

"Or you will it away," Clayton said, still frozen and staring at the big screen.

"But that only works on Kin because no matter how hard you try, you can't will all of it away. Most humans can't see past even a fraction of glamour," Rika said.

"So someone, a Kin, has seen past my glamour."

"What little you've got," Lachlin said.

"Except I haven't talked to anyone in person for four months." But that wasn't true. Every Wednesday, she'd forced herself to open her apartment door and not make eye contact with the guy delivering her groceries.

Process of elimination. There wasn't anyone else. It had to be him.

"I think we have a lead."

Morgan's delivery guy, Todd Redding, was indeed Kin and had a rap sheet involving petty theft and a few drunk and disorderlies, but nothing too serious. He lived in a small, sagging house on a street lined with small, sagging houses in a less than desirable part of town. The front yard was a mass of weeds and grass lying in matted lumps, still mostly dead from the winter, and surrounded by a rusted, waist-high metal fence. With the background of heavy gray clouds threatening rain, the whole lot looked tired and forgotten.

Lachlin and Clayton hustled down the narrow driveway to the back of the house while Gage reached for the gate separating the sidewalk from an overgrown path to the sagging front porch.

"Remember to keep your head," Gage said.

"This isn't my first rodeo, you know."

"I know." But he didn't sound certain. He drew in a quick breath and twisted the silver ring on his finger. "All right, crash course. Redding is a Naga."

"So a snake man?" She'd never expected that mythology course to be so useful. All she'd wanted was an easy elective to balance out her psychology classes.

"Exactly. A little stronger than your average human and a little faster, but not by much. What you need to watch for is their venom. If he opens his mouth, you get behind me."

"I think I can avoid being bitten."

Gage opened the gate. It groaned on rusted hinges and only opened halfway. "He can also spit it."

"Now that's disgusting. How deadly is it?"

"Depends on the Naga. Redding's venom is a paralytic, so it won't kill you right away, but if the antidote isn't administered soon enough, it'll work its way to your heart and lungs."

"Wonderful. So death by suffocation." And here she'd thought tracking violent offenders was dangerous.

Poisonous spit wasn't something handled in the marshal's manual or basic training.

Gage settled his dark gaze on her, drawing a shiver of anticipation. "You might be able to control him, but I don't want you to try unless it's absolutely necessary."

"Control him?" Lachlin's words jumped to mind. She was a snake charmer, a gorgon. "Wonderful. So I can turn people to stone and snakes think I'm the bomb. I'm never going to get a date again."

Something flashed across Gage's expression, but he turned away before she could tell what it was.

"Oh, God, please tell me I don't have snake hair."

Gage gave her a sidelong glance, a hint of a smile pulling at his lips. "It's fine. You don't have snake hair. Now come on. I'm sure Lachlin and Clayton are in position."

She followed Gage up the path to the porch and stood slightly behind him. He rested his hand on his gun, ready to draw, and knocked on the front door. Morgan matched his position, hand on gun, and strained to hear any indication someone was inside.

Nothing.

Gage knocked again.

Footsteps thudded on the other side of the door.

"I'm coming," a voice said. The door opened, and the guy who delivered her groceries stood on the other side. She recognized him from his mop of sandy blond hair and the snake tattoo on the back of his right hand.

Her gaze locked with his and his green eyes widened. Time seemed to slow and Todd's expression went from neutral to horror. A hint of fire tickled Morgan's face. She ground her teeth against it, refusing to let it grow into the terrifying inferno. It simmered and didn't billow. Maybe she could control it.

"Todd Redding?" Gage asked, shattering the moment.

With a squeak, Todd scrambled away from the door and down the hall.

Gage drew his gun and leapt after him. Morgan followed.

Todd rushed through the kitchen, yanked open the back door, and slammed into Clayton's thick outstretched arm. Todd toppled back, landing on his butt, and Clayton's enormous form filled the doorway.

Gage slowed, his weapon ready. Todd's skin turned mottled green and his face flashed into a snake's, with a stubby nose and lipless mouth. Thick flaps of skin flared from either side of his neck like a cobra's hood and he hissed, revealing a pair of wicked long teeth.

Morgan blinked. She couldn't make her mind accept this was the new reality. The fire licked at her cheeks. She jerked her gaze to the grease-covered oven door beside Todd's head and concentrated on controlling it.

Gage squared his shoulders. "Don't even think about it. Withdraw those teeth."

"You can't just barge in here." The hood quivered and a semi-translucent liquid beaded at the end of his teeth.

Lachlin cleared his throat and pointed at Clayton, who towered over Todd. The hood quivered for a second more then settled over his neck. His face wavered between human and snake and finally settled on a stomach-churning combination of the two: snake eyes and nose, and everything else human. His flesh remained pink, but dark splotches mottled his cheeks and forehead.

The blaze eased—thank God—and Morgan returned her focus to Todd again. This was her job. She now might be a monster, but that didn't mean she couldn't still be a marshal.

"I haven't done anything." Todd glanced at Morgan then back to Gage, as if he didn't want to admit recognizing her. A sure sign of guilt.

"Doesn't look like it to me." On instinct, Morgan knelt.

Gage and Clayton shifted, their discomfort that she was getting closer to Todd clear. Even Lachlin stiffened. For a heartbeat she feared she'd misjudged how dangerous Todd was. But even with the poison on his teeth ready to be spat on her—which, quite frankly, could hit her if she was standing—he didn't have the feel of a hardened criminal. And she'd met more than her fair share of hardened criminals. Nothing about Todd said he was aggressive. He'd run when he'd first seen her, he hadn't struck out even when cornered, and he certainly didn't have the build for a thug. No, his *modus operandi* was to lie, cheat, steal, and weasel—or would that be slippery as a snake? He would do whatever it would take to avoid bodily harm.

She shifted her sunglasses a fraction down her nose. Todd whimpered and inched back, bumping into the stove.

Yep. Anything to avoid harm.

And she wasn't going to think about how terrifying it was to know Todd feared her gaze. "Now you and I both know you recognized me."

"But—"

"Who'd you tell about Morgan?" Gage asked.

"No, I—"

"Come on, Todd," Morgan said, tapping her sunglasses. "Who'd you tell?"

The splotches on Todd's face paled. "I— I needed money."

"Who did you tell?" Gage asked.

"He'll kill me."

Lachlin snorted. "She'll kill you first. What do you think is more painful? Being stabbed, shot, or turned to stone?"

"I'm voting on stone," Gage said. "I hear it's slow, excruciating."

Todd trembled and paled even more.

God, she hoped Gage was playing it up.

"You obviously didn't hire the ogre. So who did? I want a name," Gage said.

"Ogre?" Todd's eyes shot wide, his slitted pupils

expanding and contracting.

Lachlin sighed. "This is getting tiresome. We're not going to get anything, so have at it, Jacobs."

"No, please," Todd squeaked. "Rentz. I owed Vincent Rentz money and when I saw her—I didn't think there was another gorgon."

"Thank you." Gage holstered his gun. "Don't leave town. We might have more questions for you."

Todd bobbed his head. His snake's hood trembled but didn't flare out.

"Good." Gage turned and motioned for her to go.

She followed him out of the house, with Lachlin and Clayton close behind her. They marched back to the vehicles and Gage pulled out his phone.

"So who's Vincent Rentz?" she asked.

"Local loan shark and Blackstone dwarf," Gage said, entering a number into his phone.

Lachlin leaned against Gage's Mustang and crossed his arms. "Except Blackstone dwarves don't usually deal in information; goods only."

Gage leveled a stern gaze on Lachlin, who pulled away from the vehicle.

"Fine. You're right," Lachlin said. "This information is worth a lot of gold, but he'd be stupid to sell it."

Gage's phone rang on speaker. "Money can make even the smartest man do stupid things."

"Goddess of all things knowable," Rika said on the other end of the line. "What can I do for you?"

"Is Vincent Rentz still running bets out of the Whale and Ale?" Gage asked.

A drop of rain hit the windshield of Gage's car.

Fingers tapped over the line. "Looks like it."

"Thank you," Gage said.

"You know I live to enlighten your life." Rika giggled and the line went dead.

"Or to make sure your credit card is declined on a big date," Lachlin said.

Clayton looked hurt. "She said it was going to be funny."

"It was funny." Gage pocketed his phone.

Lachlin scowled. "No, it wasn't."

Another raindrop hit the car.

"You weren't really interested in that aphrodite anyway." Gage turned to head around the car.

"Not the point," Lachlin said.

"No, it isn't," Gage said. "Lachlin, you and Clayton go to our ogre's residence. Maybe there'll be something there. Morgan and I will talk with Rentz."

Clayton reached for the passenger's side door on the second vehicle, a black SUV, but Lachlin didn't move. "You sure that's smart?"

Gage opened his car door and glared at Lachlin, who stiffened. The muscle in Gage's jaw twitched. If Morgan could see the air between them, she was sure it would have crackled with the tension.

"This isn't up for debate," Gage said, his voice low.

"She's untested."

"What about 'not up for debate' did you not understand?" Something deadly filled Gage's dark eyes.

A shiver swept over Morgan. Now she was certain lightning crackled between them. Gage was dangerous. If she hadn't known it before, she knew it now with certainty. She couldn't say how exactly, only that darkness coiled taut just under his skin, straining to be released, and she did not want to be on the receiving end.

Chapter 6

The tension sparked between Gage and Lachlin, growing with each passing second, and Morgan feared it would explode with deadly results. Fire licked at her eyes in response, and she fought to keep it back. She had to stay in control. She couldn't let their heightened emotions affect her.

The power radiating from Gage increased, and Lachlin sighed as if he didn't care, except the taut muscles in his arms and legs and across his back gave him away.

"Is this really necessary?" Clayton asked.

Gage remained focused on Lachlin as if he could stare him into obedience. He probably could.

The fire in Morgan's face bled over her forehead, across her jaw, and down her neck. "Please."

Lachlin glanced at her then shrugged. "Whatever." He dropped his gaze to the hood of his SUV, and sauntered to the driver's side and got in, still oozing grace and bad boy sex.

"See you at the house," Clayton said, shutting his door.

Lachlin pulled away with a squeal of tires and Morgan turned back to Gage. "What was that?"

Gage turned his attention to her and she was drowning in his eyes again. Except this time they were consuming and powerful. Even through her sunglasses she could feel the pull, like a vortex threatening to devour her soul. God, he would be amazing in the bedroom if he didn't destroy her.

Heat flooded her face at the thought and she couldn't tell if it was attraction, embarrassment, or her powers. Jeez. She slid into the passenger seat, praying he hadn't noticed.

Gage got in beside her and turned the ignition. The Mustang purred to life. The sense of power no longer radiated from him. Now the only sense she had of him was his intoxicating smell.

Which, while more pleasant than the darkness, was still a problem.

She adjusted her sunglasses and focused on the road as Gage drove. More rain dusted the windshield, but the torrent the clouds promised didn't release. "So, you wanna share?"

Gage sped through a yellow light and turned a corner, forcing Morgan to grab the door to keep from sliding in her seat. "Rentz is a Blackstone dwarf. That means he's sturdy and strong, but doesn't have any power that's likely to kill you."

"Which was why Lachlin was so against me going with you?"

Gage took another corner a little too fast, pressing Morgan against the door. "Rentz will, however, have Kin nearby who can kill you."

"Well, it's a good thing I brought my gun."

Gage stopped at a red light. "In some situations, your gun might be a liability."

The memory of her attacker turning to stone rushed through her. If turning someone to stone was possible, why not mind control? Why not body control? "But you carry?"

"I'm different."

The light turned green and he hit the gas.

"So what? I just face whoever Rentz has unarmed?" Sure, she usually did fine in a fist fight, but if she faced anyone like the ogre who'd attacked her yesterday, she wouldn't stand a chance. She liked that idea about as much as she liked the idea of being forced to turn her gun on a friend.

Gage sped around another corner, turning onto

College Avenue, one of three four-lane roads running through the heart of town. "You are hardly unarmed."

"I'm not sure my fists count against ogres and things with poisoned spit."

"I wasn't talking about that."

Heat flooded her face again, and this time she was sure it was her powers and not embarrassment. It swirled across her cheeks and around her eyes, as if the very mention of what she could do ignited it. No. He wasn't talking about fists. He was talking about her gaze. "It's hard to get answers from a statue."

Gage chuckled. "Clayton would disagree."

"Excuse me?"

"Nothing." Gage pulled into a parking spot, leaned back, adjusted the gun in his shoulder holster, and studied her. "Your ability is more than just stone. There are various levels to petrification. It just takes some practice."

She snorted at the thought. "And who gets to be the lucky guinea pigs?"

"Leave the gun." Gage got out of the car.

She put her gun in the glove compartment and followed, a bad feeling churning her gut. "Who gets to be the guinea pigs? I'm not going to practice on real people."

The image of her attacker, his cheek sliding free and shattering on the asphalt beside her head, jumped to mind. Panic swept over her. It was real. It was really real.

"And I'm not going to practice on real guinea pigs either. I don't kill cute fuzzy things."

A hint of a smile pulled at Gage's lips as he crossed the street to an old-style pub. He opened the dark wood and smoky glass door recessed into a red brick storefront. City core revitalization hadn't reached this block, and the stained brick and cracked sidewalk made the building look every bit its age—which was probably a hundred or so, when the city was first settled.

Inside was more exposed brick, dark wood, glass, and tarnished brass that said, with no uncertain terms, English pub. It was just before lunch, but only a few tables were occupied, although with the dim lighting and the tall-backed booths, there might be more customers.

With a quick scan, Morgan assessed the room. Only two men seemed dangerous, one leaning against the bar at the back and the other sitting by himself at a table in the middle of the room. Bar man was big—almost as big as the ogre had been—and with thick tusks protruding from his jaw, Morgan was sure she didn't want to get into a fight with him.

The other man was narrow, wiry, like Lachlin, except even slimmer, but there was something about him that set off her instincts. This man might not be a bruiser like tusk-guy at the back, but there was something powerfully dark about him. Not as dark as what Gage had revealed, more sly… she couldn't find the right word to describe it.

"You spot the boar ogre?" Gage asked, his voice low.

"At the bar? Yep. I'm more concerned about the man dead center."

"So am I. Lokis are unpredictable at the best of times. That could work for us as much as against us." Gage headed toward the back of the pub.

Morgan shoved back her initial denial of what he'd said—and what she was seeing. As crazy as it seemed, it was real. She really had turned her chair to stone. Right now she had to keep alert because she didn't know much of anything about this new world and that put her at a serious disadvantage. "When this is done, you and I are going to have a long talk."

"So you finally believe me. What convinced you? Turning your chair to stone? Or the poison spit?"

"Ha. You sure know how to make a girl feel better about her situation."

"I aim to please." Gage strode to the front of a booth, his arms crossed, accentuating his broad chest and well-muscled arms. Inside the booth sat a small balding man staring at the papers scattered across the worn table. His profile didn't waver into anything inhuman.

"Rentz," Gage said.

Morgan glanced back at tusk-guy, the boar ogre. He still had tusks, which meant she could see through glamour and couldn't see through Rentz's... or he didn't need one.

Rentz glanced up, a slow smile curling his thin lips, and leveled glistening black eyes on Gage. "I was wondering when you'd show up, Alexander." Rentz gestured to the seat across from him. "And I see you've brought the woman of the hour as well."

Morgan shifted under his beady stare. Warmth welled around her eyes and she concentrated on the cushioned bench back beside his head, just in case.

"Even if you weren't the only one, I'd know you were Chava's daughter. You have her look."

The warmth continued to build. From the corner of her eye, she saw the lean guy at the center table shift. She wanted to ask about her biological mother, find out what this man knew. Hell, find out anything, but she doubted she'd believe what he told her. There just seemed to be so much she didn't know about herself that everyone else did.

"I'm just disappointed you didn't invite me to the auction selling her information," Gage said.

Rentz picked up the glass by his hand and took a sip of the pale brown liquid inside. Scotch maybe? "Would I be so crass as to auction off information about the world's only gorgon?"

The only one. Which meant Gage hadn't been completely honest with her either. But now wasn't the time to ask about that.

Gage crossed his arms. "I think you'd do anything if the money was right."

"*If* the money is right." Rentz raised a finger and caught the bartender's eye.

"So who did you sell it to?" Gage asked.

"Having you show up at my doorstep isn't worth all

the gold on the planet."

The bartender grabbed a bottle from the top shelf of the back bar and sauntered toward them.

"You sold it to someone," Gage said.

The bartender filled Rentz's glass and turned to go.

"Leave the bottle." Rentz waved at the only paperless spot on the table.

The bartender set the bottle down and left. A drop of liquid ran down the neck and across the label, right through the picture of the watermill's wheel. Not Scotch, local whiskey.

"We know you've sold the information. There's already been an incident."

Morgan suppressed a snort. And by incident, he meant her apartment lobby had been destroyed, her apartment trashed, and her friend kidnapped. That was a little more than an incident.

"An incident?" Rentz sat forward, his body suddenly tense. Muscles Morgan hadn't noticed before bunched around his neck and shoulders, making him more squat and solid than before. His arms flexed and his chest seemed to expand. "There's been an incident?"

"Yes."

Rentz's eyes shimmered, light reflecting on onyx. "Believe me or not, but I haven't sold anything regarding our lovely lady here."

"Well, someone did," Gage said.

"It's a mystery, isn't it," Rentz said, his voice low.

"Yes, it is." Gage straightened. "Thank you for your time."

Rentz wrapped stubby fingers around the neck of the whiskey bottle. "Anytime, Alexander." It sounded more like a threat than an invitation.

Gage tipped his head, ever so slightly. "Rentz." Then he turned and strode back to the front door.

Morgan followed him outside onto the street. "He's keeping something back."

"He's a Blackstone dwarf. Of course he's keeping something back."

"I have no idea what that means." And the more she learned, the more she was sure she didn't want to know. Except she had no choice. Even if she returned to her sequestered life in a new apartment, this new reality would still be there. This reality seemed determined to force itself on her. She couldn't close her eyes and pretend it wasn't real.

Gage marched past her to the curb. "I can give you a full briefing when we get back to the house, but I'm not sure *brief* is the right word."

"Wonderful. Please tell me Rika's set up a wiki for this, an 'Everything Someone Needs to Know about Kin'."

"There's a set of encyclopedias in the library. No one's spent the time to scan it into a computer."

"That big, hunh?"

A hint of a smile pulled at his lips. "And full of strange words, too. You might need help reading it."

Hell, yes. "I'm sure I can handle it." Jeez. She had to keep her head. She didn't know anything about Gage or anyone else for that matter. "We should focus on our current situation."

The traffic broke and they headed across the street back to the Mustang.

"Blackstone is a dwarven clan. They align themselves with the Darkling Kin."

"I'm afraid to ask. Darkling Kin?"

Gage rounded the front of the vehicle, pulling his keys from his pocket. "Darkling—" His gaze locked on something up the street and his eyes widened.

Tires squealed and a silver truck tore toward them, a machine gun pointed out the passenger window.

The man holding the weapon morphed between human and cat-monster. Black fur slid over his face then receded back to human. Slitted pupils glared at her.

"Morgan!"

The gun. It was pointed right at her.

Shit.

Chapter 7

Gunfire exploded around Morgan. She dove over the Mustang's hood, crashing to the sidewalk. Adrenaline pounded through her. Her thigh stung, and her sore ribs ached.

Gage fired back. Two quick shots. More machine-gun fire pounded into the car, rattling Morgan's teeth. She glanced over the hood at the cat-man in the truck, who gave off another burst of gunfire aimed at her.

She jerked back under cover and Gage fired again. Glass shattered, tires squealed, and the silver truck roared away.

Gage sprang to his feet, his gun aimed at the retreating

vehicle. It fishtailed around a corner and disappeared. With a growl, he punched the ruined hood of his car. "That's it. You're staying in the house."

"The hell I am." She wanted to catch whoever was responsible even more now. "I'm not some wilting flower who curls into a ball at the first sign of trouble."

"That wasn't trouble, that was a MAC-10."

"Yes, it was." Heat rippled over her eyes and she didn't care. Bring it on. She was tired of hiding and being scared of herself.

"Pull yourself together."

He knew. Somehow he could tell her eyes burned and that she didn't care. "Stop telling me what I can or can't do."

"Then start listening to reason." He straightened and the air around him crackled. Energy snapped across her skin. Darkness. Power. His eyes captured hers, pulling her into an abyss.

The heat in her eyes flared. She wouldn't be scared into obedience. A small part of her quivered at the thought. She should be terrified of what she saw in Gage, but the Medusa's fury was stronger than fear. No one told her what to do and no one got in her way when a friend was in danger.

But Gage was so powerful.

And so the hell was she.

More energy snapped around her. More heat flooded her face.

Something chirped.

The heat faltered and Gage's power wavered.

The chirp came again. With a growl, Gage pulled his phone out of his back pocket. "What?"

Morgan tried to blink back the fire. As much as she wanted to just let go and rage, it wasn't going to help anything.

"Thank God you're alive," Rika said. "9-1-1 calls reported a drive-by at the Whale and Ale and mentioned two people being shot at with a description of your car."

"We're fine," he growled.

"Whoa, Mr. Growly. Pull it back. Don't want to give Morgan the wrong impression," Rika said.

The hint of energy crackling around him vanished so fast it took Morgan's breath with it.

"The police are on the way. I've informed Detective Wright it's part of a case and you'll send him the paperwork later."

"Thank you," Gage said, his voice still dark. "We're coming in. Get Lachlin to pick us up since I'm sure the crime scene unit will want my car for a while."

"As you wish." The line went dead.

The muscle in his jaw twitched and he pocketed the phone. "You don't know anything about what you're dealing with."

"I know my friend is in trouble and someone's trying to kill me. I know I have the training to deal with that." She blinked back the rest of the heat in her eyes. "Let's agree the situation is dangerous and that I'm not going to let you bench me."

"I could lock you up."

"You could. But I think you'd rather have me on your side than against it." It was a risk to draw the line so clearly like that. She still didn't know half of what was going on, but if she'd overheard that first conversation with Lachlin right, back at the house, Gage wanted her on his team; locking her up wouldn't accomplish that.

"Fine. Let's get back to the house and figure out what we've got."

"Good. And what we've got is the truck's license plate." She grabbed her gun from the glove box.

Gage barked a quick laugh. It wrapped around her senses like his scent did. "Silly me for doubting you."

"I'm sure you won't make that mistake again."

His smile turned sly. "No, I won't."

Lachlin picked them up, saving them from Wright's less than congenial mood, and they returned to the house, heading straight to the situation room. The computer was still working on cleaning the background on the photo and Rika was on a different side of the computer table, her fingers flying across a touch-sensitive keyboard on the screen.

"I ran the plates on the silver truck, but it was reported stolen earlier this morning. Any luck with Rentz?" she asked.

Gage leaned against the table, arms crossed, his gaze locked on the now-blurry photo on the big screen. "Nothing. He says he didn't sell Morgan's identity and got quite angry when I mentioned something had already happened."

"Which means he was sitting on the information, waiting for the most opportune time to sell," Morgan said. At least some things didn't change between the Kin and humans, but Morgan didn't know if that was better or worse. It said she was important and she didn't have a clue as to what or how or why... or the answer to any other question she could come up with.

"Typical." Lachlin dropped into a chair beside Rika, making the action look smooth and sensual.

Clayton took the chair beside him and stared again at the photo.

"So did Todd Redding try to double-sell the information? Did Rentz lie about sitting on it? Or has someone in Rentz's house betrayed him?" Rika asked.

Morgan bit back a growl and plopped into the chair opposite Lachlin. "And that still doesn't help us find Kate."

"No, it doesn't," Clayton said.

"Neither does this." Rika swiped phone records onto the big screen. "There's nothing unusual with either Todd Redding's or Daryl Matas's phone records."

"Any of the numbers the same?" Lachlin asked.

Rika tapped the table, but nothing changed. "No."

"Maybe try doing a search on the numbers for the last couple of months with any of Rentz's known associates." Morgan bit back a sigh. It was a long shot, since they didn't even know if Rentz was involved, but it was something to try.

"As well as our Kin profiles of known felons," Gage said.

"Which leaves us with what?" Lachlin asked.

Morgan shoved out of her chair. "A whole lot of nothing." She couldn't just sit there. She had to do something.

"Gage and Lachlin will figure this out," Clayton said. "They always do."

She paced to the door at the back. Beyond lay the hall leading to the rec room where she'd first met everyone. And beyond that, the bedroom where she'd woken this morning. How could her life have been turned upside down so fast?

Except it hadn't been fast at all. It had started four months ago when she'd turned her attacker to stone. The image of his cheek cracking and breaking free flashed across her mind's eye. Why couldn't she just get the damned image from her mind. Even her scar ached now.

She drew in a ragged breath. Kate needed her. Now was not the time to lose it.

One of the phones in her pocket vibrated. It had to be the kidnapper's, since she hadn't turned the ringer on her phone off. She pulled it out and turned to Gage.

"Track it," he said.

This was it.

Rika typed into the computer. "Keep them talking."

The phone vibrated again and she hit the call button. "Jacobs."

"Bring the contents of evidence box 19780324-2 to the corner of 5th and Lexington in one hour," a tinny computerized voice said.

"An evidence box? I don't have access to that." What did they want with an evidence box?

"You're a U.S. marshal. I'm sure you'll figure something out. Box 19780324-2. 5th and Lexington. One hour. Come alone. Do I need to tell you what will happen to your friend if you're not there?"

"Let me talk to Kate."

"Bring the box."

Rika motioned to keep going. She needed more time.

"I want to talk to Kate."

"The box." The line went dead.

"Not enough time," Rika said. "They were somewhere downtown in a ten-block radius."

"Too many people to check," Clayton said.

Morgan shoved the phone back in her pocket. "What do they want with an evidence box? And one from 1978?"

Gage glanced at Lachlin, his expression dark, but Morgan couldn't figure out if it was at the situation or something else.

"It's just a ploy to make us think they're not after Jacobs. They couldn't very well demand she exchange herself for a human." Lachlin hooked a now shoulder-length lock of hair behind a normal human ear.

She really wasn't going to get used to seeing people two different ways at any given time.

"I agree. But we need to play along until we get Morgan's friend to safety," Gage said.

"And maybe they picked this case number for a reason." Morgan paced back to the table. She could feel the fire in her eyes, but it was just a flicker, a pinpoint, waiting for her to call on it. "With any luck, it'll give us a clue as to who's behind this."

"They could have picked any old number," Lachlin said.

"They could have." Gage adjusted his sidearm in his shoulder holster. "Regardless, we need that box. Looks like I've got a call to make."

Lachlin sat forward. "The chief of police is going to love you. How many times have you called in the last couple of months throwing your FBI weight around?"

"No more than necessary."

"One of these days, he's going to put his foot down and refuse you," Lachlin said.

"He hasn't yet." Gage pulled his phone from his back pocket. "And really, if he refuses, I'll get to put you to work to use your charm on him."

Lachlin rolled his eyes. "That'll be the day."

Gage flashed his cocky grin. "Let's see if today's that day."

Chapter 8

The property office storing police evidence was in a warehouse attached to the back of the new police services main office on the east side of town. The four-story building had been constructed about six years ago as a part of the city's revitalization plans—when the block the previous station had been on had been purchased by a developer for a new condominium complex and shopping center.

Gage parked his replacement car—a navy midsized sedan—in visitor parking near the property office's public entrance, cut the engine, and turned to her. "I feel compelled to remind you to let me take the lead on this."

"You think I won't behave?" She didn't know if she should be insulted or flattered at the comment.

"Obedience is not in your genetic makeup. At least, not on your mother's side." He reached for the door handle.

"About that."

He gripped the handle but didn't open the door. "When this is cleared up, we'll talk."

"Did you know her?" She'd never really wondered about her biological parents before. Her adoptive parents hadn't hidden that fact from her, and she had a great relationship with them… or at least she had before she'd locked herself in her apartment for four months.

And now she'd just learned she had the equivalent of a terrible genetic disorder, for a lack of any better way to put it. Whether she wanted to or not, she needed to know everything she could about her birth parents, particularly the part of her that could kill someone.

"She was a member of our team, but I'm not sure I really knew her." The muscle in his jaw flexed, and he opened the door. "Now's not the time to talk about this."

"No, it isn't." But very soon, once Kate was safe, it would be.

She got out of the car and walked with Gage to the front door. He opened it for her and she entered a small glass and chrome lobby. Before them sat a black and chrome reception counter, guarding the thick security door leading to the property room, and beside them, in front of the large front window, sat a stainless steel bench inset with blue fabric cushions—that didn't look thick enough to cushion anything.

A Santa Claus look-a-like, in a police officer's uniform, shifted on his stool behind the reception desk and smiled at them. "What can I do for you?"

Gage showed his identification. "Special Agent Gage and Deputy United States Marshal Jacobs. The chief of police should have called and said we were coming."

Santa's smile faded and he ran a hand over his neatly trimmed beard. "Yes. You need to check out an evidence box from 1978?"

"A case we're working on might have ties to it." Gage leaned against the counter.

"From 1978. That's a long time ago," Santa said.

"Yes, it is, and this is time sensitive."

There were those words again.

Gage tapped the counter's shiny surface. "The chain of custody form, if you please?"

"Yes, of course." Santa pulled a file folder from the wire rack beside him. It looked like the chief of police had indeed called ahead, although Morgan had no idea what Gage had told him to get such a fast response.

Gage filled out the form and Santa pulled up the box's details on his computer.

"The box is in row 12." Santa hit the button under the desk, unlocking the security door, and Gage opened it. Beyond was a ten-by-ten holding area and a metal gate, halfway open, with Detective Wright on the other side.

Wright's eyes narrowed. "Special Agent Gage."

Gage stepped into the area between the doors. "Detective."

"What brings you to the property office?" Wright asked.

"Checking out a box from '78," Santa said through the window beside them.

"Really. 1978? Any chance this has something to do with the drive-by shooting?"

"Yes to '78," Gage said. "No to the shooting."

"Well, aren't you Mr. Popular, then." Wright glanced at Morgan. "Still interviewing for that job, Marshal?" he asked, his tone clear he didn't believe anything that had been said so far.

"Any luck on the perps who trashed my apartment?"

"Prints can take a while," Wright said.

"Yes, they can." Sometimes too long, at least in the case of fugitive apprehension. "I'm sure you're doing everything you can." Maybe if she played nice, he'd leave.

His eyes narrowed even more. Guess what she said could have also been taken as an insult.

"And all of us should get back to work." Gage shifted so Wright could pass.

"Special Agent. Deputy Marshal," Wright said, the words sounding like insults. He shoved past them and stormed out of the warehouse.

Santa looked confused, but Gage rushed Morgan

inside and out of sight before he could ask questions.

At row 5, out of earshot from Santa, Morgan glanced at Gage. "So you and Wright have history?"

"You could say that."

"You know, it usually helps to make friends with the police." She turned down row 12.

Gage followed. "Making enemies was never my intention. Sometimes my job requires me to take situations out of people's hands. The detective Wright replaced knew that. Wright is new to his position and just hasn't accepted that yet." Gage stepped closer to the shelf. "This is 1978. October."

"We're looking for March."

Morgan scanned the shelf sections. September… August… There, at the bottom. "Found it." She slid it out, reaching to open the lid to see what was inside.

Gage pushed her hand away and took the box. "Great. Now let's get it out of here."

"Aren't you curious about what's inside?"

"We likely won't have time to recreate what's in the box and we can't risk the kidnappers already knowing what the box should contain, so we can't give them a fake box."

"But knowing what they're after might help us identify them."

He hesitated for a split second then set the box on the floor and opened it. "You're right. But just enough to give Rika something to work with. We don't have a lot of time." He must really want to get Kate to safety. Although Kate really wasn't his goal. It was Morgan and getting her on his side. He'd been clear about that from the beginning, so if Kate was her concern, Morgan supposed it became his by default.

Inside the box was a case file, a bloody dress shirt and pair of pants, one shell casing, and a jar of gray sand; all properly bagged and labeled.

Morgan picked up the jar. The label read 'granite dust'. She couldn't imagine why the kidnappers might have picked this case.

Gage pulled out his phone, took pictures of a few pages of the file and the contents of the box, then dialed. "Lachlin. I've sent you some photos of the contents of the evidence box. Get Rika to run them and see if we come up with anything."

Lachlin said something, but Morgan couldn't make out his words and she put the jar back in the box. Maybe Lachlin was right and the box had been picked at random.

"All right. We'll meet you in that alley on 4th in ten minutes." Gage ended the call, put the lid back on the box, and tucked it under his arm. "Now come on. Let's get your friend back."

Chapter 9

Gage pulled into an alley off 4th street, stopped beside Lachlin's SUV, and got out. Morgan followed. The rain had started in full, pouring a cold heavy shower on them, but the narrow alley sheltered them from the worst of it.

Lachlin eased from the vehicle, all grace and danger. Morgan caught a glimpse of Rika in the front passenger seat working on a computer tablet before the door closed.

"Clayton is in position." Lachlin handed Gage two wireless earpieces.

"In this rain? Poor Clayton." Morgan took the offered earpiece. "Tell me he's at least got shelter." Sure, sometimes the job required uncomfortable conditions, but that didn't mean she didn't feel guilty about Clayton having to deal with it because of her.

"The weather won't bother him." Gage inserted his earpiece. "What's the layout?"

"It's under the expressway. The closest building is a hundred yards away across a parking lot. An old factory that Rika says hasn't been in use for about ten years. Doesn't look like there are any great sniper perches, particularly if you want to stay out of the weather," Lachlin said. "I can't sense anyone in the area, so they likely haven't shown up yet."

"And you're certain they're Kin and they're after me?" Morgan slid the earpiece with microphone into her ear. She had to give Gage's team credit; they had topnotch technology.

"There's still a chance this is connected to your job as a marshal, but I'd say it's awfully slim," Gage said.

"Which means whoever we're facing will be Kin." And that meant Morgan had no clue as to who or what she was up against. "Did Rika have any luck drawing a connection between any Kin and the evidence in the box?"

Lachlin glanced at Gage then back to Morgan. "No. They must have picked a number at random. Just like I said earlier."

Gage shifted but didn't give him a dark look as Morgan would have expected. He was all business now. No combative banter and no glare-downs. "The odds that they'll bring Kate to the exchange are low. Morgan, be ready for an attack the moment you step from the car."

"Got it." She fought the urge to reach for her gun. Gage had said it was dangerous for her to have it, but she wasn't going to face a monster without it. It was all she had—since there was no way in hell she was going to turn someone to stone.

"And remember, whoever shows up, we need them alive so we can find Kate," Gage said.

"Sure thing." Lachlin shrugged and got back into the SUV. Morgan couldn't tell if he was going to listen to Gage's order or not.

Gage held out the key to the sedan to her. "We'll be right there."

His scent wrapped around her and her attention locked on the key. She'd have to make contact with his hand to get it.

"If things go south, get to cover." His tone was soft, soothing.

She glanced into his bottomless eyes. "Is this really happening?"

She didn't know where the question had come from, or the sudden doubt. Nothing seemed real anymore. It hadn't since the attack in an alley much like this one, four months ago.

The image of her attacker's face shattering on the pavement flashed through her mind. She had done that. She really had.

Gage took her hand, sending a shiver sweeping up her arm. He pressed the key into her palm. "I know everything seems strange right now."

She snorted. "To put it mildly."

"When this is over, I'll help you figure it out." He stroked a finger along the arm of her sunglasses, brushing her cheek. His scent wrapped tighter around her. Strong, sensual. Another shiver slid over her. He would help her. That meant spending more time together. Hell yes to that.

"Let's do a mic check everyone," Rika said over the earpiece.

"Lachlin, check."

"Clayton, wet."

"Gage, here."

Yes, he was.

Warmth swept over Morgan's face and it wasn't the warmth of her unwanted abilities. She took the key and eased away from him. "Morgan, check."

"Remember, the goal is apprehension. Lethal force is a last resort." Gage reached for the back door to Lachlin's SUV and turned back to Morgan. "Don't get killed."

"Done this before, remember."

"Not this, you haven't," he said.

The SUV window rolled down and Lachlin leaned out. "Get your ass in here. We need to get into position before the kidnappers show up."

"Not here yet," Clayton said.

Lachlin rolled his eyes. "I can sense that."

Morgan got into the sedan and waited for Lachlin to pull out onto the street. She could do this. Gage and his team would protect her before the kidnappers could use whatever abilities they had on her. And if it was another Naga, all the better. Spit didn't fly well in a storm.

She drove over to 5th Street, followed it a block down to Lexington, and parked under the raised expressway cutting through the west side of town.

Now came the waiting.

She hated waiting.

The wind picked up, pelting the rain against the car in sideways torrential waves. If the weather wasn't so bad, she'd get out and pace.

Damn, she needed to move, burn energy, do something.

She couldn't just sit there.

She checked the time on her phone.

"You just got there," Gage said. "Fidgety already?"

"Yeah, I'm a nightmare on stake-outs. But it's worse since—"

"Since your powers manifested?" Rika asked.

"Not surprising," Lachlin said. "It's a gorgon thing. Perpetual motion and all that. Kind of like a shark."

"Gee, thanks." She wasn't sure she liked being compared to a shark and didn't know if it was an improvement over snake charmer.

"That was meant as a compliment," Lachlin said.

Someone cleared his throat, the sound deep and raspy

in her ear. "Only a few more minutes," Gage said.

"And here they come," Lachlin said. "I've got two, feels like an ogre and a cat. No human. Unless she's enspelled, she's not in the truck."

Morgan glanced out the window. The silver truck roared off Lancaster into the far end of the lot under the expressway. It tore through puddles, washing aside garbage and debris, racing toward her.

Morgan tensed and cracked open the door, ready to jump. But the truck's tires locked. It swerved, slid perpendicular to her, and skidded to a stop in a rush of water and gravel. The driver's door opened and the man with tusks from the Whale and Ale climbed out.

Well, that explained how the kidnappers knew about her. Rentz's muscle had probably overheard Todd trying to sell the information on her.

"Take this easy," Gage said. "Eyes open for that MAC-10."

"I know what I'm doing." She eased from the car.

Rain pelted her, soaking into her jacket and jeans and beading on her sunglasses.

"Got the box?" the man asked. His tusks wavered into sight and his skin turned thick and gray.

"Where's Kate?"

"Have you looked in it?"

Morgan squinted through the rain on her glasses. "We're here to do an exchange. The weather isn't getting any better. Where's Kate?"

"Has Gage looked in it?" Tusk-man asked.

"He's not going to hand her over," Gage said.

"You're sure she's not in the truck?" Morgan asked, keeping her voice low and praying Tusk-man couldn't see her mouth move in the storm.

"Unless she's enspelled, no," Lachlin said.

"Clayton, get ready," Gage said.

A hulking shadow shifted near the pillar behind the truck.

"Did Gage look in it?" Tusk-man growled.

"Why do you want it? What are you trying to cover up?" Damn it, she really couldn't see right with the water on the lenses.

"It's not what I'm trying to cover up, snake charmer."

"Then who?"

"He's stalling," Gage said.

"Where's Kate?" Morgan yanked off the sunglasses.

Tusk-man threw his head back and roared.

"Move, now," Gage said.

Lachlin's SUV tore into the lot. Machine-gun fire exploded out the passenger window of the silver truck at the pillar instead of the SUV. Clayton staggered forward. Bullets pounded into his chest and he dropped.

Oh, God.

"Man down!" Morgan drew her gun, but Tusk-man charged her. She fired off a shot, hit him in the shoulder, but he didn't even flinch.

He hurtled toward her, roaring. She leapt out of the

way, her shoulder and back hitting the gravel. She scrambled to her feet, but Tusk-man lunged, grabbing for her. She staggered back and fired again. No effect.

"Lachlin to Clayton," Gage said.

"Where's Kate?" Fire licked at her eyes and she forced it back. She had to stay in control.

Tusk-man sneered. "You'll never know."

Gage raced toward them. He slid over the hood of the car and energy crackled around him. Thunder in the clouds above answered, booming around them.

Tusk-man grabbed for Morgan. She sidestepped his attack and slammed the butt of her pistol into his cheek. He lurched back—a weakness—and she struck again.

Behind him, darkness gathered around Gage. He drew his hand up and a whip of fire and night burst to life. He snapped the whip at Tusk-man, snaring his leg.

Tusk-man screamed, and Gage tossed him into the pillar beside the truck. More machine-gun fire spat from the truck. It peppered a line across the hood of the sedan, and Gage and Morgan dove for cover behind the vehicle.

Lachlin darted to the passenger side of the truck. The man with the machine gun—Cat-man from earlier— twisted, aiming for Lachlin. Lachlin wrenched the barrel down. Gunfire slammed into the gravel beside him.

Tusk-man staggered to his feet and pounded on the back of the truck. The tarp on top flew to the side and a monster, an honest-to-goodness monster, rose from the bed. Dog-like, it snarled, revealing a mouth full of sharp teeth. Water slicked its hairless body and it put an enormous paw on the side of the truck bed. It snorted, and flame and smoke licked its nostrils. Embers burned in its eyes and it locked its gaze on Morgan.

"Holy shit," Lachlin said. "A pit beast."

The creature jerked its head toward him.

Gage scrambled to his feet. "Run."

The beast swiped at Lachlin, its claws digging rents into the top of the cab. Lachlin scrambled away and machine-gun fire slammed into the pillar beside him.

Gage's whip crackled back to life. He snapped it at the beast, which sprang from the truck, and the whip missed. Lachlin bolted to the pillar and Gage cracked the whip again, slicing the beast's side.

The creature roared and surged at Gage and Morgan. Gage snared his whip around the creature's front paw. It tripped and slammed into the hood of the sedan, crushing it. The beast growled and tossed the car to the side. Morgan scrambled back, more fire swarming across her cheeks.

Stay. In. Control. It was too dangerous for her to release her power.

Gage's whip tangled around the creature's legs and he tugged it off balance.

"Get out of here," he yelled at her.

"No way in hell." She didn't abandon anyone in a fight, no matter how insane it got.

Cat-man fired another blast at Lachlin, pinning him

behind the pillar, and Tusk-man ran in the opposite direction, deeper under the expressway. He was getting away and that could put Kate's life in jeopardy.

Morgan bolted after Tusk-man, but a roar made her glance back. The beast yanked at the whip, throwing Gage into the ruined car.

He staggered to his feet. The whip flared above his head and flew toward the beast, wrapping around its neck.

Something big lurched at the corner of Morgan's eye, and Lachlin's SUV, with Rika at the wheel, gunned forward. It slammed into the beast and drove it into the pillar. The creature howled and sagged, and Morgan could only pray it was dead.

She turned back to Tusk-man, pushing herself to run faster. She had no idea how she was going to stop him— bullets didn't seem to work—but letting him go wasn't an option.

He scrambled through a hole in a chain-link fence and slid down a grass and gravel hill into a gully. Morgan raced after him.

Rain beat at her, cold and stinging, and the wind tore at her hair and clothes. She ground her teeth and ran harder. She could catch him. She would catch him.

The gully ended in a large water runoff tunnel, and Tusk-man ran headlong into it. Morgan followed, gun ready, and twilight engulfed her.

A large figure lurched beside her. Tusk-man. He

grabbed her gun and wrenched it from her hands. It clattered deeper into the pitch-black tunnel.

She slammed her fist into his face. His head snapped back and something crunched. She punched again, but he surged close, blocking her swing with his shoulder. He clamped a large hand over her throat and inched her up until her toes skimmed the ground.

She'd come full circle in less than twenty-four hours, with some monster choking the life out of her.

He sneered and flicked his tusk across her cheek. Hot pain burst over her face.

"That was for my sister."

"What the hell are you talking about?" An inferno burned across her eyes. No. Control it. If she killed him, she might never find Kate. She clawed at his fingers, but just like the other ogre, she couldn't break his grip.

He jerked her forward and slammed her against the wall again. Pain exploded in her chest and the inferno in her eyes pulsed. Please, no. For Kate's sake.

He slapped his hand over her eyes. "Many Houses will be avenged today."

She thrashed against his grip. The blaze threatened to explode. She couldn't hold it back. God, she had to. "Where's Kate?"

Her heart pounded and her limbs grew heavy. Flames beat within her, filling her head and pouring into her chest. She had to let it go, but it wouldn't release. Not with her eyes covered. She was burning alive from the inside out.

"My House will be avenged."

"Not today," Gage said, his voice muffled. He sounded in front of her and in her head all at the same time.

The hand on her face jerked away. Her eyelids flew open and locked on Tusk-man as he seized the front of Gage's shirt. The fire erupted from her eyes, rushing through her in a ferocious blast.

Tusk-man screamed. He twitched once, twice, then stopped. A crack boomed around them and a fissure snaked through Tusk-man's arm. Another crack and another. Fissures sliced through his face, his torso, his legs.

He moaned. Oh God, he was still alive. Bile burned the back of Morgan's throat, but the power consumed her. It poured, wave after wave, and she couldn't stop it. She struggled to close her eyes, cover them with her hands, do something, but she couldn't move.

"Please," he gasped.

"Morgan, control it. Focus," Gage said.

But she couldn't. The fire kept spewing from her, growing stronger and stronger with each rapid pulse of her heart.

The fissure in Tusk-man's arm ruptured and his hand snapped off, shattering on the ground. He moaned again and his other arm broke free.

God, please. Make it stop.

Her body trembled, but the power held her rigid. At any moment, she would explode from it.

Tusk-man's left leg crumbled and he toppled over, shattering on the floor. Gage staggered forward and Morgan's gaze locked on him.

He gasped and stiffened.

No, please.

"Morgan."

Stop. Just stop. Why couldn't she shut it off? She fought to close her eyes and strained to move, to breathe, to do anything.

Gage's face turned gray. The promise of his own power swarmed around him, gathering, threatening. Her magic flared at the thought. She had to live.

No. Not if she murdered Gage.

She had to stop.

Please.

Something moved at the corner of her eye. She jerked toward it and Lachlin's fist smashed into her face. The power vanished.

Another blow cracked against her cheek.

She staggered back. The tunnel tilted around her and flooded with darkness.

Chapter 10

Morgan woke with a start, sending a wave of nausea washing through her. Pain radiated through her chest and head, and the adhesive from a bandage pulled at her cheek. Her neck ached once again, and her eyes were on fire and filled with grit.

Her heart skipped a beat. Her eyes were on fire. She squeezed them shut, but the wave of power she'd felt before didn't build. It wasn't the same kind of fire as the magic. It was the stayed-up-too-late, opened-her-eyes-in-the-ocean, and rubbed-sand-in-them kind of fire.

"It was a fucking pit beast," Lachlin said, his voice sharp but hushed. "He gave them a pit beast."

He sounded in front of her and close. Beneath her cheek, the floor or blanket or whatever she was on was coarse and smelled of new car.

"Just a lesser one," Gage said. "I'm more worried about the evidence box. It seems he wants to send us a message as well as eliminate her."

"I prefer email."

A vehicle door opened. She had to be in the SUV, since the car had been destroyed.

"I'm going to check on how Rika's doing with Clayton," Gage said. "Call me when she wakes. We still need to find her friend and I have no doubt that if these guys don't check in with someone soon, Morgan's friend will be dead."

"She's dead either way," Lachlin said.

"Maybe the kidnapper is smart enough to keep her alive for leverage."

"We can only hope."

The SUV door clicked closed and Lachlin sighed. "I know you're awake."

She opened her eyes. She was in the back of the SUV with the backseats flipped down out of the way to make more space. Lachlin sat behind the steering wheel, his pale gaze locked on hers. She couldn't help wondering when he'd realized she was awake and how much of that conversation he knew she'd overheard. But if he wanted to bring it up, she figured he would.

She rubbed her jaw. "My face hurts."

"Sorry about that."

"No, you're not."

His expression darkened and he pursed his lips. He *was* sorry. His attention jumped to the window and Morgan followed his gaze. The rain had stopped, or at least it had stopped blowing sideways. Clayton leaned against a pillar while Rika squatted in front of him and Gage stood beside him.

Lachlin turned away from them to stare out the cracked front window. "You're dangerous."

"Yes, I am." And that terrified her. She could have killed Gage. She would have killed him if Lachlin hadn't knocked her out.

"But you haven't gone crazy and you held it together when faced with the pit beast."

"I hear it was just a lesser one."

Lachlin barked a soft sensual laugh. Everything about him, even when he was being a prick, was sexy. "You really are a snake charmer."

"I wish you'd stop calling me that."

He offered her a lazy smile. "I mean it with my best intentions."

"Which is awfully close to your worst intentions, I'm sure." Outside, Gage shifted and Rika slid a pair of tweezers out of Clayton's chest, removing a bullet. "Shouldn't he be in the hospital?" Or dead. And where was the blood? Admittedly, his jacket was black and soaked with rain, but he should be lying in a pool of blood given how many times he'd been hit.

"He'll heal. It'll take a while, though. Bullets disrupt the magic sustaining him."

"I don't understand what that means."

The smile returned. "I know you don't, Kitten." He set her gun on the armrest between the front seats, opened his door, and got out.

"Prick."

"Wouldn't you like to find out." He sauntered away, oozing bad boy sex.

Morgan bit back a sigh, grabbed her gun, and eased out of the SUV but didn't chase after him. Instead, she holstered her sidearm and leaned against the vehicle. Its front end had crumpled against the pillar and blood slicked the crushed hood. The pit beast lay in a heap between the SUV and the pillar, still a terrifying monster of teeth and claws even if it was dead.

This was her world now. Whether she wanted it or not, this was her new reality.

She snorted. Reality was overrated.

White lightning shot through her chest and she hugged her ribs. They really hurt, which meant they had to be at the very least cracked. But Gage was right. If they didn't figure out where Kate was, the chances of finding her alive, or at all, grew even more slim.

Gage glanced up from Rika and Clayton. His gaze caught Morgan's and she pulled her attention to her feet. She *was* dangerous, and it was foolish of her to have forgotten that. She'd just been so caught up with the thrill of the hunt and her determination to save her friend. She could never afford to forget that again. Next time Lachlin might not be around to knock her out. In reality, she should be locked up for everyone's safety.

Footsteps crunched in the wet gravel, and Gage's army boots stepped into sight.

She didn't know what to say. How did someone apologize for almost turning a person to stone? 'I'm sorry' just didn't seem enough.

His hand eased into sight, holding a pair of sunglasses. "You lost these."

"I think I need more than a pair of sunglasses." A locked psych ward would probably be a good idea.

"A little bit of practice might help as well."

"More than just a little." To do that, she had to accept what she was. And really, that was the only way she could guarantee anyone's safety. Locking herself away only made her a bomb that could explode at the slightest provocation.

"We'll help you with this." He shifted closer, and his sensual scent wrapped around her. "I'll help you."

She flicked her gaze up—she couldn't help herself—and met his bottomless brown eyes. A glimmer of the power and darkness she'd sensed earlier burned there. He was dangerous, too. Perhaps more dangerous than she was.

He didn't flinch from her gaze, holding it instead,

holding her. She could have killed him back in the tunnel and she could kill him now, but he remained focused on her as if he knew her. Or perhaps he just knew what it was like to be her. Something she wasn't even sure about anymore.

She dragged her attention to Clayton and the others. "Is he going to be all right?" She couldn't believe she was asking that, but now the impossible was entirely possible.

"He'll be out of commission for a while. His magic will have to focus on healing his body, but he'll be fine. The only thing that can drop him is a powerful magic-voiding spell, or an inferno."

"Really?"

"He's a golem. A magically animated wooden statue to be precise, although there's more to him than meets the eye. He's got too much personality for just a golem."

"Of course he does." Now she really needed to read that encyclopedia back at Gage's house.

"Now come on." He pressed the sunglasses into her hand. "We need to figure out where your friend is, and we're running short on time."

"You should send me back to the house."

"That's what Lachlin would say."

"In this case, I think he's right." She put on the glasses but didn't feel reassured.

"I'll do that once we figure out where your friend is. Right now, let's focus on finding anything that might help. Come on." He headed to the silver truck.

Focus on the job. She could do that. Kate needed her to do that. She drew in a steadying breath, sending stabbing pain shooting through her chest. Right, don't do that. "Do we have identification on the two men?"

"The boar ogre's identification was destroyed, but he was definitely Rentz's muscle back at the Whale and Ale."

"Which means Rentz could still be involved in this."

"Yes. But so far we've found no connection with the bakeneko."

"Bakeneko?"

"A cat-like race. Most of the myths about them are from Japan, hence the Japanese name, but they aren't exclusive to the area." Gage opened the silver truck's driver's side door. Cat-man, the bakeneko, sagged on the passenger side, his eyes wide and empty. There was nothing indicating how he died. "And unfortunately, the only way Lachlin could stop him was to blast his mind."

Morgan glanced over the truck to Lachlin. He looked up as if he knew she was watching him and offered a wry smile. When this was over, she needed to find out what everyone could do. Clayton could survive being shot repeatedly in the chest, Lachlin seemed to know what she was thinking, and Gage… there was more to Gage than he let on. But all of them gave off an air of secrecy, a desire not to be exposed, and she had a feeling she'd have to tread lightly when asking questions.

Gage pulled out a wad of receipts and used burger wrappers from the tray beneath the steering wheel. "And we have no idea if this is from the kidnappers or the actual owner of the truck."

"So we have nothing." They had less than nothing.

Something dinged and Rika straightened. "The algorithm on the photo is done."

Please let there be a clue.

Rika handed the tweezers to Clayton, who didn't look hurt at all, rushed to Lachlin's SUV, and pulled out her tablet. "We got something, but I'm not sure it'll help."

Morgan and Gage joined her. The picture of Kate was now brighter and sharper. The wall behind her was still dark, but it was clear it was cinderblock flecked with hints of peeling paint. There had to be something here, some small detail that would indicate where Kate was.

"There's a hint of a door along the right side." Rika drew her fingers across the tablet, made the picture larger, and shifted it to reveal the edge of a heavy door.

Gage leaned closer. "That door is too industrial looking for a house basement."

"So warehouse, maybe?" Rika said.

Morgan stared at the picture. There was something on the door, the line of a symbol, or something.

"It would have to be abandoned or owned by one of the kidnappers for no one to have noticed anything," Gage said.

"What's that on the door?" Morgan asked. It curved. Two lines running side by side with one... no, two lines running between them.

Rika enlarged the picture even more.

"What is that?" Gage asked.

There were more than two lines. They only had the edge of the image, it was barely noticeable, but it looked like… "A waterwheel."

"Doesn't the old Black Mill distillery use the waterwheel as part of its symbol?" Rika asked.

"Yes, and we saw a bottle of that on Rentz's table." Which didn't make Rentz more or less of a suspect. Tuskman, the ogre, would have seen the bottle as well. Anyone familiar with the north side of town knew the old Black Mill distillery was on the river's edge because the symbol was painted on the side of the building. Rumor had it the company was planning something with the abandoned property, but there'd been mention of that from the moment Black Mill had moved to their new facility closer to the expressway fifteen years ago.

Rika tapped on her tablet and pulled up an aerial map of the area. "With the property that size, it would be easy to keep someone there without drawing attention."

The distillery's building was on a full acre of property, now mostly overgrown, on the edge of town. It sat in the river's narrow valley below the Rosemount Bridge, and its closest neighbor was a farmhouse on the other side of the river and up the rise.

"It's the best we've got. Rika, you stay with Clayton and continue searching the bakeneko for anything else. Lachlin, Morgan, you're with me."

Morgan turned to the SUV and its destroyed front. "We have no vehicle."

Gage strode to the truck, opened the passenger side door, and pulled out Cat-man's body. "Yes, we do."

"This is a terrible idea," Lachlin said. "She shouldn't be coming with us."

"I agree. I'll stay with Rika and Clayton." As much as she wanted to be a part of this, it wasn't safe for Gage or Lachlin.

"This isn't up for debate. You can keep it together, Morgan. Besides, if they have a second pit beast, Lachlin and I will need all the help we can get." Gage got into the truck and slid across the bench to the driver's side.

"Speak for yourself," Lachlin said, but he motioned for Morgan to get in. "Really, the odds of them having a second pit beast are impossible."

"Still not odds," Clayton said.

Lachlin glared at Clayton, but it felt half-hearted. Morgan climbed in and Lachlin followed, wedging her between him and Gage.

She was not going to think about how close they were.

Gage turned on the ignition and gunned it onto Lexington. If they were wrong about the distillery, Kate would likely be dead, but it was the only lead they had. And if Gage was wrong about Morgan, he could be dead as well.

Chapter 11

Morgan got out of the truck. Rain ran down her neck beneath her collar and beaded on the sunglasses. They were going to be a real pain in this weather, but she wasn't going to risk taking them off again. Gage had parked at the mouth of the long, forested road leading to the distillery, so they could approach on foot and hopefully have the element of surprise.

"I borrowed a nearby satellite," Rika said over the earpiece. "I can't keep it for long, but I can confirm there are no heat signatures outside the building."

"I'm sensing that as well," Lachlin said.

Gage drew his sidearm. "What about inside?"

"There are two near the northwest corner," Rika said.

Lachlin closed his eyes and frowned. "One is definitely human. She's conscious, angry, and planning. I don't think she's hurt, or if she is, it isn't consuming her thoughts. I can't tell what the other one is. I'm getting nothing from him other than a presence."

"Well, that narrows the list down to about two dozen Kin," Gage said.

Lachlin snorted. "And let's not forget the handful who I can't sense and won't show up on Rika's scan."

"So even though we've checked, there's still a possibility we're going in blind and we have no idea what we're up against?" Morgan drew her sidearm.

Gage raised an eyebrow.

"That's about right," Rika said. "And I've got nothing more from our known kidnappers that could help."

"All right, eyes open, ready for anything." Gage glanced at Morgan's gun again. "Lachlin, take the rear. Morgan, in the middle. Your focus is Kate. Once we find her, get her out of there. We'll cover you."

She nodded and turned her attention to the thicket of branches from the winter-barren shrubs and trees, searching for signs of assailants or traps. Going in with Gage and Lachlin was a terrible idea. She couldn't control her powers and she was just as likely to kill one of them or Kate, as she was to kill the kidnapper.

At the thought, fire licked around her eyes. Damn it. Stay calm. She could do this. She really had no choice in the matter.

She hustled up the road with the guys, ignoring the rain as best she could, her senses straining. A hundred yards down, the road curved and opened into an overgrown lot with the sagging distillery building at the back.

Dead stalks of weeds and grass claimed most of the wide gravel area in front. The building, a three-story structure, sagged, tired and weather-worn, at the river's edge. The remains of the waterwheel, the symbol of the distillery, jutted over the rushing water, swollen with the day's rain. Gray boards covered the few windows on this side of the building on the first floor and half of the windows on the second floor.

It didn't look as if there was an available entrance on the front and they would be exposed to anyone looking out a window if they approached. Their team wasn't large enough to split for multiple entries and their time was short. The longer they took, the greater the chance any remaining kidnappers would realize their friends had failed—if they hadn't figured it out already… and if, in fact, the heat signatures inside were a kidnapper and Kate.

"Can't see the east wall," Lachlin said.

"Only other logical place for a door." Gage inched closer. "Are both heat signatures on the northwest side?"

"Yes," Rika said.

"Good. Fast and quiet." Gage motioned them into action.

They rushed across the lot to the south face of the building, their footsteps crunching in the gravel.

Adrenaline beat through Morgan and the fire in her eyes flickered in response. But the usual thrill of the chase was missing. Kate was in danger…

And Morgan *was* a danger.

They reached the shelter of the south wall, which provided some respite from the downpour. Lachlin examined the forest behind them while Gage glanced around the corner. Morgan strained to hear anything inside. Nothing. The only sounds were the rush of rain and the hiss of wind in the trees.

"Emotionally, nothing has changed inside," Lachlin said, his voice soft.

"Loading dock, thirty feet down." Gage jerked his chin at the corner.

"What are the odds they'll be expecting that?" Morgan asked. If whoever planned the kidnapping had a clue, they would be prepared for Gage and his team. If the kidnappers were amateurs, the odds were less, but anything was possible.

Lachlin shrugged. "With the way our luck has been going, I'd say whoever's inside knew we were coming the moment we hit the driveway."

"Glad we have Mr. Positive on our side," Morgan said.

Gage shot her a wry smile. "He has his uses." He rushed around the corner, forcing Morgan and Lachlin to follow in silence and keep formation.

A concrete slab jutted from the side of the building about thirty feet away, as promised. Beyond it, half a wooden shed leaned against the building. The other half was a pile of wood and stone debris.

Gage hopped onto the loading dock platform. Morgan eased up behind him, mindful of her ribs. Sagging, broken doors stood partially open, revealing a dark interior. She tipped her sunglasses down. Machinery and shelves and things Morgan couldn't identify in the gloom loomed around them. She wasn't going to be able to see anything with the shades on, which meant she was going to have to go in without them. Just great.

"This way." Gage motioned them forward.

Morgan shoved the sunglasses into her jacket pocket. She followed Gage, creeping into a vast, three-story space toward a massive, towering vat. Pipes ran from it, snaking above them, disappearing into the darkness.

Pale bands of gray light cut this way and that from the boarded and broken windows, making it difficult to see what was in the deepest shadows, and rain rattled on the tin roof, making it impossible to hear the soft sound of anyone hiding nearby.

Something flickered at the edge of her vision. She glanced back and Lachlin frowned. The gray light from the partially open door framed him, accentuating his sleek build. Fog curled along the floor, snaking around his feet.

Except the fog didn't look right… maybe? It seemed too dark for fog, more like smoke, and yet in the gloom it was hard to tell.

Lachlin's frown deepened and his gaze followed hers to his feet. His eyes widened. "Ah, shit."

The smoke turned into a shadowy clawed hand, seized his ankle and jerked up, tumbling him forward into Morgan.

She grabbed him, her ribs screaming in protest, but the smoky hand yanked him back, throwing him to the ground.

The rest of the smoke coalesced into a human shape, a man about Lachlin's size. Red eyes glowed from a cloudy face with a sharp nose and elongated canines.

Morgan pointed her gun at the smoke-man as Lachlin twisted and kicked. Lachlin's foot passed through the creature's body, drawing a laugh.

Gage grabbed Morgan's shoulder and pulled her back. "It's a smoke demon. I'd say your friend is here."

Lachlin jerked against the hand still holding his ankle. Gage's fire whip crackled to life and snapped through Smoke-man's arm. The demon's body lost shape and the smoke pulsed, expanding as if with each breath. Lachlin wrenched free and scrambled back. The smoke billowed and split, forming two smoke-men.

"Get moving." Gage cut his whip through both smoke-men. They burst apart and reformed.

Lachlin fired into one of them, the bullet passing through it. They laughed together and the one Lachlin had shot leapt at him, a solid fist cracking him in the jaw.

The other split, becoming two and split again.

Now there were five.

Gage swept his whip through them. They blew apart, reformed, and rushed at Gage and Morgan, laughing, billowing, fists and claws and faces solid with smoky bodies.

One smoke-man slashed at Morgan. She raised her arm to block, but Smoke-man's wrist swept through hers. She jerked back, and his claws grazed her cheek, ripping off the bandage. He slashed again and she scrambled out of the way. Fire burned across her eyes and she struggled to keep her power at bay.

Energy crackled around Gage. The flames burning along his whip flared. Two smoke-men grabbed for him. He ducked and snapped the whip up, cutting one in the face. It howled and burst apart.

So they could be hurt. If she timed it right. But the creature split into two more smoke-men and swept back at Gage.

"We have to get Kate out of here." Gage snapped his whip again, but it passed through the smoke-man. "Northwest corner."

Morgan scrambled back from another flurry of fists and claws. Her power burst across her face.

Not. Now. She couldn't risk hurting Gage or Lachlin. She had to find Kate.

But the smoke-men were pushing them away from the northwest corner.

Lachlin dodged a strike to his side and twisted out of the way of a punch to his face.

The smoke-men multiplied again. There were now too many to count.

Lachlin kicked and punched, but his strikes never hit anything solid. Gage's whip sliced through them, blowing them apart, but they reformed just as fast.

A smoke-man grabbed for Morgan. She twisted out of the way, agony stabbing through her chest. His nails raked across her arm, drawing deep rents in her flesh through her jacket. The fire in her face burned hotter.

"Help, Morgan," Lachlin gasped.

"I'm trying."

"No, petrify their asses."

The blaze in her eyes flared. "I can't. It's not safe."

"Screw safe."

The smoke-men billowed around them. She could barely see Lachlin through the writhing mass of smoke.

"No. Get to Kate and get her out of here." Energy crackled around Gage but didn't manifest into anything, as if he couldn't focus it, couldn't bend it to his will save for in the form of a whip.

A smoke-man shoved her into the hands of another one. She wrenched free of his grip. Her power raged through her, setting her whole face on fire.

"Morgan," Lachlin said.

She glanced at him; the smoke-men had dragged him to the floor and were slashing at him. Her magic flared.

The floor beside him cracked.

"Get Kate," Gage growled.

From the corner of her eye, Gage's whip sliced through the creatures on Lachlin, who scrambled back to his feet.

She forced her attention on the smoke-man before her. The creature swiped at her. She ducked.

Gage snapped his whip again. "Now."

The smoke-men in front of her burst apart and she bolted through them. Claws slashed at her, snaring her jacket. She twisted out of it and raced toward the northwest corner of the building.

Smoke-men flew from the group after her. Gage's whip flashed beside her and one of the smoke-men flew apart. The other seized her arm and jerked her around.

Lachlin was being pulled down again, his face and arms bleeding. Blood also oozed down Gage's face. One of the smoke-men had his whip hand and was dragging him down as well.

The fire in her face exploded. She jerked her gaze up and the pipes above groaned.

Power poured from her eyes. The pipes cracked and broke free, shattering on the floor in a roar of powder and stone shrapnel.

She couldn't see Gage or Lachlin and everywhere she did look, things groaned and cracked, becoming stone.

"Gage? Lachlin?" She pulled her attention to the smoke-man beside her. He froze, hand poised to strike, and screamed. Stone swept over him; the smoke hardened and fractured.

"Get Kate out of here," Gage said.

And control her God damn power. If she didn't get a hold of it, she'd kill Kate. That thought only made her power surge. She wanted to squeeze her eyes shut, take a moment to focus, but there wasn't time. Smoke-men surged toward her. Gage's and Lachlin's breath rasped over the earpiece.

She had to pull it together. She dashed toward the northwest wall. She would control her power. It wouldn't control her.

The fire flared in protest and she sucked it back, her will strengthened by desperation.

She raced across the dark room and around a second enormous vat. Ten feet away were a smoke-man and Kate. She was still gagged and her right eye still swollen shut, but her left eye was clear and determined. Behind them was the door from the photo with the distillery's faded and peeling logo. Above was a rickety set of metal stairs. Two possible means of escape.

He slashed the rope binding Kate's arms to the chair, yanked her to her feet, and poised his claws against her neck.

"Not so fast, snake charmer." He kicked the chair to the side and snarled.

Morgan skidded to a halt. Instinct kicked in and she aimed her gun at him.

"You don't think that'll do anything, do you?" His red eyes simmered and a forked tongue flicked out, like a lizard testing the air.

Morgan fought to keep her attention off Kate. The fire burned around her eyes, threatening to burst free. "Let her go."

"Or you'll what?" Smoke-man snickered. "You're surrounded."

"Get Kate out and we won't be anymore," Gage said in her ear.

Morgan's gaze jumped to Kate. A band of gray light cut across her pale face, accentuating the line of blood crusted to her cheek. She clung to the hand at her neck— the very solid hand—and pressed against a solid chest. Her body tensed and she gave an ever so slight nod. It was risky, but she was trained and so was Morgan. They knew how to deal with this.

Heat flared in Morgan's face. She sucked it back.

Kate shifted, exposing more of Smoke-man's shoulder, and Morgan fired.

Smoke-man jerked back, the bullet passing through him, and Kate wrenched free. She punched at his face, but her hand flew through his head. She staggered forward, off balance. Morgan leapt at her, grabbed her wrist, and yanked her away.

Smoke-man roared, billowed, and multiplied.

Kate stumbled back, her eyes wide.

"We have to get out of here." Morgan turned to run

back to the door, but smoke-men swarmed behind them. Smoke-man was in front of the other door, which left the stairs and a quick prayer the door at the top would be open.

She tugged Kate to the staircase. Smoke-man lunged at them, his claws raking across Morgan's back. She bit back a scream. Magic burned over her and she fought to keep it at bay. Kate yanked the gag down, scrambled up the stairs, and Morgan followed to the door at the top. Please let it be open. Please let it be a way out.

Kate threw herself at the door. It flew open and they raced onto a catwalk that wrapped around the building. Rain pelted them, soaking Morgan in seconds, and wind snatched at her hair and clothes.

"Outside," Morgan said. "On a catwalk."

Something roared inside the distillery and an enormous line of fire, much like Gage's whip, leapt through the roof, its flame flaring and snapping in the rain. Smoke-man swept up behind them, screaming, his face twisted with rage and pain. Rain hissed through him, tearing away pieces of his smoke. He trembled and turned solid. Rain washed over his face and dripped from his nose and chin.

Morgan shot, hitting him in the chest. He rippled and the bullet burst from his back, slamming into the metal doorframe behind him.

Kate grabbed Morgan's shoulder. "What the hell is that?"

"I have no idea. And I don't plan on sticking around to find out."

"Agreed."

They bolted along the slick catwalk around the corner. It led to the broken waterwheel and nowhere else. They were trapped.

The building groaned and another chunk of the ceiling fell in.

"Gage? Lachlin?" They were still inside.

"Almost at you," Gage said.

"Good, because we've got nowhere to go."

"Keep him in the rain. I'll be there."

Morgan fired another shot at Smoke-man.

It swept through him.

"Can you climb down?" she asked over her shoulder.

"Maybe," Kate said.

"I'll hold him off." She fired another shot, but it didn't stop him. She was running out of options.

The fire pulsed in her face, driving down into her body.

"It's a shame your mother isn't around to experience the same grief I felt when she killed my son." He billowed, forming and reforming as the rain ripped at his edges.

"I had nothing to do with that." She hadn't even known her mother.

Kate hung to the slick railing, straining to reach the windowsill just below her. Morgan needed to buy more time. Just a little more until Kate could get to safety.

"Even just one of your kind is a plague on Kin." Smoke-man's tongue flicked out. "You can't be controlled. Even your friends know that."

"What are you talking about?"

"You're a monster among monsters." Smoke-man growled and leapt at her.

Morgan fired again. The bullet passed through him, and he swiped at her, knocking the gun from her hand. She staggered back and punched. Her hand went through his face.

Rain hissed through him. He swirled and reformed, his hands raking at her face.

She grabbed his wrists and held him for a second. He turned to smoke, swept through her fingers, and swiped at her cheek. She twisted to the side. White-hot pain slid across her jaw and the fire in her eyes exploded in response. Her gaze locked on Smoke-man, but red light flared from his throat.

He threw his head back and laughed, revealing an orb the size of a marble, hanging from a gold chain around his neck. "Your powers don't work on me, snake charmer. I have a protection spell." He tapped the marble with his claw and sneered. "And now you can die helpless like all your mother's victims."

He shoved her and she slipped on the slick metal, toppling onto her butt. Pain spiked through her chest. Her power slammed into the distillery wall. It turned to stone and cracked.

Smoke-man lunged and she scrambled back. His claws snagged her pant leg and he yanked her forward. She kicked at him with her free foot, but it went right through him. The rain followed, washing away pieces of smoke. He growled, his face tight with pain.

She kicked again. Rain pulled at more smoke, but he reformed. Behind him, Gage ran into sight. He snapped his whip, sweeping through Smoke-man, who reformed but just a fraction slower each time. Gage had said keep him in the rain. Rain broke up smoke, or fog, or whatever he was. Rain dissipated it.

Morgan glanced at Kate, now clinging to the windowsill. Below them, the river rushed, brown and frothy. He'd turn to smoke before they hit the water and, with her luck, float to safety. But above her, on the roof, stood a rusted rooftop water tank.

Smoke-man drew his hand back to strike. Gage's whip sliced through it and Smoke-man howled. He seized the front of Morgan's shirt and jerked her up and around, putting her between him and Gage.

She twisted, trying to get out of the way, but his claws raked across her chest. Fire burst from her eyes and she threw it at the water tank.

Metal squealed and groaned.

Morgan grabbed Smoke-man's hand, wrapped in the front of her shirt. Smoke-man drew back again for another strike. Gage's whip sliced through Smoke-man's raised hand, and he turned to smoke, save for the hand clutching her.

The water tank shattered and water crashed over them. Smoke-man screamed. He exploded into smoke, and the water and wind tore at him, ripping him to shreds.

Morgan staggered back and released his dismembered hand. Rain pelted it, pulling pieces of smoke from it until it dissolved.

The inferno in her eyes dissipated and she sagged to her knees. Below her, Kate crouched in the grass, her face white and eyes wide.

Gage's muddy boot toe inched into sight beside her. "The smoke demon is dead. You and Kate are safe."

But she wasn't really safe. Not from herself. And there was no escaping this new reality.

She blinked back the remaining fire and glanced up at him. She was just going to have to deal with it. "We need to have a long talk."

A hint of a wry smile pulled at Gage's lips. In that moment, he looked entirely human and entirely delicious. "Yes, we do."

And while she wasn't sure she was going to enjoy the conversation, she was certainly going to enjoy the company.

Chapter 12

Morgan sat with Kate in the back of an ambulance, aching all over and with no idea what to say to her friend. Across the gravel lot, the distillery building stood in shambles. The roof and two walls had collapsed, and Morgan had no idea how Gage was going to explain any of this to the police. Who, along with Rika, an ambulance, and Detective Wright, had arrived about fifteen minutes ago.

Gage had insisted Kate and Morgan go first with the paramedics, even though Lachlin looked like he'd gotten the worst of the fight. The men had stood back with Rika, keeping under the shelter of an ancient pine while the paramedics bound Morgan's cuts and checked out Kate, and the rain poured around them. They'd had a brief conversation with Wright and, from the way the detective had stormed off, he wasn't happy. He barked something at the two uniformed officers who'd arrived with him, and they got back into their cruiser and left. Wright marched back to his car and after about five minutes left as well. Now the paramedics were talking with Gage and Lachlin and from the crossed arms and scowls on both sides, they were refusing treatment.

Rika threw her tiny hands into the air and stalked off, muttering about men. Morgan would have to agree. She didn't want to go back to the hospital, but from the sounds the paramedics had made, a few of the cuts on her body probably needed stitches and she definitely had broken ribs.

"So which one is yours?" Kate asked.

"Excuse me?"

Kate jerked her chin out the ambulance door. "The hot one or the hot one? And can I have the other?"

"Gage? Lachlin?" Well, Morgan couldn't deny they were nice to look at, each in their own way. But hell, she'd just found out she was a monster. That was more than enough to deal with right now.

"He's why you haven't called in four months, isn't he?"

"Who?"

"Whichever one of those two you're sleeping with."

Heat flooded Morgan's face and this time it was full-blown embarrassment. "I'm not sleeping with either of them."

"Then can I?" Kate flashed a mischievous smile. She was teasing… maybe.

Morgan rolled her eyes. "I barely know them."

"Then it's perfect."

"You're terrible."

Kate leaned forward. "And you didn't call." All the mirth was gone from her voice.

The wind gusted, spraying rain into the ambulance. It beaded on Morgan's cheeks, and she wiped it away—and just rain, nothing else, really. She'd abandoned everyone she knew, save for maybe Izzy, who was too far away to endanger. But if she understood the explanation for the Kin's glamour, she couldn't explain why to anyone. Well, she could, but no one would believe her, or they'd think she was crazy. She still didn't know if she wasn't crazy.

No, she wasn't crazy. The world was.

Morgan blew out a long breath. "I needed to get my head together."

"And you had to do that without your friends?"

"I thought I did."

Kate raised an eyebrow. "How's that working for you?"

"I'm sure Izzy has told you it hasn't been working very well at all." And now the question was, what would Morgan do about it.

"She's worried. I'm worried."

Lachlin said something and one of the paramedics shook his head and strode back to the ambulance.

"But if I'd known you'd hook up with two smok'n hot guys, I would have intruded on your life sooner," Kate said.

"You intruded? Weren't you just kidnapped? I would hardly say you had anything to do with that. And why haven't you freaked out about all this?"

"Oh, I plan to live in denial with this one for the rest of my life." A darkness flashed across Kate's eyes. Her reaction to the smoke demon flashed through Morgan's memory.

"You saw it?" Morgan concentrated, trying to see if Kate had a glamour, but her appearance didn't change.

"I don't know what I saw, and I have no intention of losing my job because of a stress-induced anything, and you're not going to tell the boss either."

"Cross my heart. But we'll have to tell him something."

"What will your FBI hotties say?"

"I don't know."

Gage turned to the ambulance, his gaze catching Morgan's and sparking a warmth of attraction within her.

"Whatever it is, I'm sure the boss will have him fill out the paperwork in triplicate," Kate said.

One of the paramedics hopped into the back of the ambulance. "All right, ladies. This bus is going to the hospital. I recommend you both come along for the ride."

"I've got Marshal Jacobs," Gage said, striding up to them. Somehow in the fight he'd lost his jacket and the rain plastered his already tight T-shirt to his well-muscled chest.

"I bet he does," Kate said under her breath.

Morgan resisted the urge to glare at her friend, even in jest. "I'll meet you at the hospital."

"And then you, me, two glasses of merlot, and a long talk."

"I don't recommend the wine," the paramedic said.

"Trust me. If you knew what my last twenty-four hours had been like, you'd recommend the whole damned bottle."

Morgan straightened, pain radiating through her. She bit the inside of her cheek, trying not to show it, and eased out of the ambulance. Gage shut the door, and it drove away, leaving her in the rain with Gage and his enticing scent. Even in the rain, his scent wrapped around her.

She shoved her hands into her pockets. She didn't know what to say or ask. She wasn't certain about anything anymore. "So."

"So." Runnels of water streamed down his face, accentuating the hard lines of his cheeks and jaw.

"Do we stand out here until one of us gets a cold?" she asked.

"I can't get colds."

"Fantastic. What else should I know about you?" The wind tugged at her hair and she hugged herself against the chill that had soaked into her clothes.

"Your friend will be fine," he said.

"Not what I asked."

"The details of the events will change in her mind. By the time she wakes tomorrow, anything Kin related will be changed to something her brain can handle."

Swell. So much for having a possible outside ally in all this. "The glamour is that powerful?"

"Yes, it is." He dug his boot toe into the mud and gravel. "Rika says the DNA came back and all four of the kidnappers can be linked to cases the team worked on with your mother. Looks like Rentz wasn't involved after all."

So this had everything to do with a biological mother she'd never met. "How many more of these people are out there?" But she knew the moment she asked the list could be endless. Just like her job as a marshal, criminals had friends and families. Kin had... well, kin.

"You're among the most powerful of the Kin. There will be those who'll want to control you, and those who, if they can't control you, will want you dead." Gage twisted the ring on his right index finger. "You'll be safe with us."

"And by with us you mean...?"

"At the house. With the team... on the team." Which

was what he'd said when she'd first overheard him talking with Lachlin. But did he want her on the team because he genuinely cared or because he was one of the Kin who wanted to control her? He ran a hand over his hair, slicking it back. "When your mother died, she asked me to find you, to protect you."

"From all those crazy Kin out there who want me dead just because I'm a gorgon?" She wanted to ask about the case in the evidence box, but she didn't know if she'd get a straight answer. She needed outside information to corroborate his story. As much as he was hot and smelled really good, that didn't mean she could trust him.

"And protection from one Kin specifically." His gaze locked onto hers and she was drowning in his eyes.

"Who?"

"The Kin who killed your mother." He blinked, releasing her for a heartbeat and capturing her again. "It was just supposed to be a precaution. But when I realized you'd come into your powers, I knew you were in danger."

"Because I'm a gorgon?"

"Because only a gorgon can stop him." He twisted the ring again. "He's why you're the last of your kind."

"And you think this attack, these kidnappers, are connected to him?" The ruined distillery building groaned and another piece of wall crumbled.

"There's no proof of that."

But his conversation with Lachlin in the SUV said they knew differently and somehow the case in that evidence box was connected.

"But you suspect it?"

"Anything is possible."

A hint of fire licked at her eyes and she forced it back. His dancing around the subject could just be another attempt to protect her. It might not mean anything.

Except her instincts said there was more to this story than Gage was saying. Yet everything he'd done since she'd met him had been to protect her. Besides, she knew nothing about the world she'd suddenly found herself in. At the very least, she needed to power-read that set of encyclopedias at Gage's house.

"You have no reason to trust me," he said, as if reading her thoughts. "But your mother wished for me to protect you."

Morgan snorted. "You're doing a terrible job at that. I just got the crap beaten out of me."

"And you almost turned me to stone. I'd say we're even. Come on." He jerked his chin to the new SUV where Rika and Lachlin waited. "Let's go home."

To a new and terrifying life. One where she was surrounded by monsters of myth. One where she was a monster herself. But she didn't have much of a choice. She needed to learn to control her powers and her best bet was with Gage and his team. Besides, living by herself was too dangerous for everyone.

Fine then. At least she wasn't crazy and didn't have snake hair.

Bring it on.

Turn the page for a look at

The

Medusa Files

CASE 2:
HEART OF STONE

Chapter 1

The body lay at the end of the alley in a pile of garbage bags. Crime scene technicians, the medical examiner, and police officers swarmed the area in what Morgan could only hope—for the victim's sake—was organized chaos. She sat in the back of Lachlin's new SUV, parked across the street, waiting.

For what... she didn't know. She'd been in Gage's library, almost finished the second volume in the encyclopedia set on Kin—not that she'd remember half of what she'd read—when Gage had knocked on the doorframe and told her to grab her U.S. Marshal's identification. They had a call. Whatever that meant.

Now they were at the edge of the business district, parked at the side of the road across from the alley, waiting. She hated waiting. It was just after lunch but the patio of the restaurant beside the alley was packed with onlookers. So, too, was the front step of the warehouse-turned-fabric-shop on the other side, keeping the few uniformed officers instructed to preserve the crime scene busy.

"So what's the deal?" She pushed a wild curl from her face, the movement drawing a dull ache from her ribs. Seven days ago, when everything had changed and she'd learned she was a monster of myth, her ribs had been broken. Now, they were barely cracked, thanks to a flighty woman—literally, she had gossamer wings—who'd been laying her healing hands on everyone on the team.

Gage glanced back at her from the front passenger seat. A set of three red scars ran across his cheek, accentuating the hard lines of his face. His dark eyes captured hers for a heartbeat, even through her sunglasses, sparking a shiver of attraction.

She drew in a steadying breath, but his heady scent of musk and mint filled the SUV, wrapping around her senses. Really, it was the April sun warming the inside of the dark vehicle and nothing else.

But boy, would she like to do some laying-on-of-hands with someone.

She shoved that thought aside. It was entirely

inappropriate, particularly since she didn't really know anything about Alexander Gage, FBI, or anyone else on the team, regardless that she was now living with them on their small estate in Old Town. Man of Mystery didn't even begin to sum it up.

Their conversations—hell, her conversations with everyone—so far had been brief. There were times when she felt she was alone in that big house. Gage had said something about giving her space and time to adjust, and everyone had respected that and avoided her. Or were they avoiding the inevitable conversations about how dangerous her new powers were and the mother she'd inherited them from?

Perhaps this invitation out was Gage's way of saying he was ready to talk.

She adjusted her shades and turned her attention back to the alley. "You said we had a call?"

"Routine procedure. I thought it would be a good introduction to what the team does," Gage said.

Lachlin, who'd been surprisingly quiet in the driver's seat, snorted. "Because we need three people to confirm a corpse. You could have taken this one yourself."

There was the Lachlin she'd first met. Arrogant, confident, always ready to question Gage, and oozing bad-boy sex. If Gage was the marine, Lachlin was the high-end art thief.

"Right now, no one does a job solo. Not even a routine procedure." Gage brought his phone to life.

"Looks like Rika has emailed the particulars so far." He pulled up a mug shot and scrolled to the next page. "Our victim is Scarlet Worley. She's a sylph and therefore Kin, which means we need to follow up on her death."

"You follow up on every Kin death?" Morgan shifted. She'd been sitting too long. She needed to get up, stretch her legs. The urge to move, which had been building for days now, was apparently a side effect of being a gorgon. Something else she was just going to have to get used to.

"We always follow up to determine if a death, particularly a murder, is Kin-related," Gage said. "If it is, we take it from the police."

"Since they can't handle the truth." Lachlin chuckled.

More like they couldn't remember the truth with the Kin's magical glamour making it impossible for non-Kin to remember anything Kin-related.

"Scarlet has a handful of prostitution priors so this is likely just the result of bad choices." Gage slid his phone back into his pocket. "We'll wait until the medical examiner has taken the body then check in with the crime scene unit."

"But most importantly, we'll wait for Detective Wright to vacate the premises," Lachlin said.

"If you'd rather we didn't, we can go now." Gage reached for the door handle.

"No." Lachlin shrugged and tucked a strand of black hair behind a pointed ear. It wavered and turned into a blunted, human one. "Why waste the energy?"

Morgan glanced at Gage, but his image remained the same. Dark, short-cut hair, strong jaw, normal ears. If he had a glamour hiding his true appearance, she had yet to see past it like Lachlin's. "I haven't even been around for a week, and even I know eventually you boys are going to need to figure out what to do about Wright."

"But now is not the case." Gage twisted the silver ring on his right index finger.

Lachlin rolled his eyes. "This isn't even a case. No doubt Scarlet's less-than-desirable lifestyle ended with an entirely human demise."

"Wow, great investigation techniques. Glad to know the assumption is alive and well." Not that Lachlin probably wasn't far off. People who lived hard lifestyles often died by them.

"The snake charmer has already figured everything out. Why am I here again?" Lachlin asked.

"Because I live to make your life miserable," Gage said.

Detective Wright got into his two-toned brown station wagon and drove away. The medical examiner packed up the body and headed out, and most of the police dispersed, leaving the crime scene technicians to their job.

Gage got out of the car. Morgan and Lachlin followed.

"Most of the crime scene unit is familiar with us." Gage straightened his black leather jacket.

"So it's just Wright Lachlin is afraid of?" Morgan asked, unable to resist the jab.

"Oh, Kitten, try a little harder next time." Lachlin flipped waist-length hair over his shoulder and marched across the street, leaving them on the curb. His hair shortened to shoulder-length as she watched, then lengthened again. God, she was never going to get used to that.

The traffic light at the other end of the street turned green. Half a dozen cars headed their way and she and Gage lost their opportunity to cross with Lachlin.

"We've been working with the crime scene unit for a couple of years now," Gage said. "They're used to us. But Wright transferred from Chicago six months ago, and the relationship we have with the police is a delicate one, slowly built on trust."

Morgan glanced at Gage over the top of her sunglasses. It was a dangerous move since the sunglasses helped to keep her unwanted ability to turn people to stone at bay—or at least that was the theory—but she couldn't help herself. "Did you just say trust? Everything you tell the police is a lie."

"We tell them what they'll remember. Trust me, it hasn't been easy trying to figure out what the glamour will change in their minds and what it won't." The traffic cleared, and Gage and Morgan crossed the street, heading to the alley. "It's easier to work with people on an ongoing basis if Lachlin hasn't charmed them stupid with his magic."

As if hearing his name, Lachlin glanced up from his

conversation with one of the crime scene technicians and rolled his eyes at them. They stood at the mouth of the alley, their body language casual, as if what lay beyond the threshold from street to alley wasn't there. Lachlin was one of the first things Morgan had looked up in the encyclopedia. Gage had said Lachlin was fae, but the entry hadn't been helpful at all.

Fae had a variety of abilities and not all fae had them: magically charm—usually humans although a rare few could even charm fellow Kin—spellweaving, mind reading, body control, and soul control were just a few on a long list. She did know Lachlin could sense people around him, and there was something about him that pulled at an irrational, primal part of herself—a part she was determined to ignore—but that was it. Anything else he could do was pure speculation.

The man he talked to wavered into a shaggy ape-like figure then flickered back to human. She couldn't begin to imagine what type of Kin he was, but the very fact he was Kin might explain why Gage and his team had a good working relationship with the crime scene unit. The technician's gaze landed on Morgan. His eyes widened and stayed big.

Wonderful. She couldn't help but wonder if Gage had lied about her having snake hair.

She ran a hand over her mess of silver curls, which was already fighting the elastic she'd thrown around it. Without a doubt, stray curls had broken free of the ponytail and were sticking out in a wild halo. Really, she should just give up trying to tame it, just like she'd given up on trying to dye it—the damned locks resisted even that. But while she might now be a gorgon, she was still a girl and cared about how she looked.

She slid her gaze to Gage. Yep, she cared how she looked, damn it. And that was stupid, potentially dangerous, and still inappropriate. She really needed her friend Kate to set her up on a date or something. Anything to get her out and distract her.

"So what have we got, Nick?" Gage asked.

The technician, Nick, continued to stare.

"Deputy U.S. Marshal Jacobs," she said, pulling out her badge—the one she wasn't supposed to be using since she still wasn't back on active duty—but perhaps if she spoke like a normal person, he'd start acting like a normal... whatever he was.

Nick blinked. She raised an eyebrow.

"I believe Special Agent Gage asked you a question," she said.

"Jeez." Lachlin shook his head and strolled deeper into the alley, where the body had been.

Gage cleared his throat. "Nick?"

Nick shook himself. Hair bristled on his face then sucked back, hidden by his glamour. "Yes. Right. Pleasure to meet you, Marshal." He started to hold out his hand, hesitated, then let it drop and turned his attention to Gage. "The victim was stabbed with a large blade, maybe a chef's knife or something. Once in the heart, and all the way through. Her purse is missing and so is any jewelry she might have been wearing. We IDed her from her fingerprints and she's in the system for prostitution."

"So a mugging gone wrong?" Morgan asked.

"That would be my assessment," Nick said without looking at her. "Looks like the normal human kind of monster. I'll send my guys for coffee and wait by the van. You can have the alley for the next twenty minutes or so."

"Thank you." Gage headed deeper into the alley and Morgan followed.

"So that's it?" she asked.

"Pretty much. We need to check the scene for any residual magic, since Nick is a sasquatch and not attuned to it, and the rest of his team are human, but that's about it."

"So some Kin can sense magic and others can't?" She'd just assumed that because Kin were magical creatures they could sense magic—even if she wasn't entirely sure what magic was.

"Not all are attuned to it. If you weren't half human, you'd be able to detect just about everything."

"But I am half human. Which means—?"

He turned his dark, bottomless gaze on her and held her captive for a second. Then he blinked, releasing her. So many mysteries with this guy. "I have no idea if you'll be able to detect anything or not."

"And if I do, what will it look like?"

"It differs from person to person. Some feel it like a breeze across their skin. Some see it like light flickering at the edge of their vision. It all depends."

"Wonderful. So we won't really know if I can sense magic and how until it happens. If it happens." Why couldn't there just be someone who knew all the answers about her and could just tell her what was what. While her powers hadn't gone crazy since fighting off the smoke demon who'd kidnapped Kate, Morgan didn't doubt it was because she'd been nice and quiet and relatively unstressed for the last seven days. But there was always the risk heat would burn across her eyes and she'd turn everything she looked at to stone.

As if summoned by her fear, a hint of heat licked around her eyes. She sucked in a calming breath and focused on the black graffiti on the alley wall. Last time she'd lost control, she'd killed a man and almost killed Gage. She never wanted to do that again.

The heat cooled. Nothing turned to stone and crumbled. One point for her. Now all she had to do was get through the rest of her life like this.

Garbage littered the alley, still wet from the showers earlier in the week. Halfway down, by a heavy back door, stood a dumpster, its dark green paint scored and flecked. It had all started four months ago in an alley just like this.

The memory of the man who'd started it all flashed into her mind's eye. He'd slammed her head against a dumpster and rammed his knife into her chest.

She fought to blink back the memory, but it filled her, running its horrifying course.

His face had cracked. His cheek had slid free and shattered on the asphalt. He'd turned to stone and crumbled.

And now she knew turning to stone had been agonizing.

Sweat slicked her palms and the back of her neck, and her breath burned through her too-tight throat. She'd killed him. Slowly. Painfully. She was a monster. An honest-to-goodness monster of myth. Oh, God.

Her legs trembled—her whole body shook. She was going to go crazy. She already was. It was impossible. Not real.

She knelt and pressed a palm to the asphalt, focusing on its bite into her skin.

That was real.

She was real.

This new reality was real, too. She'd been handling it just fine for the last week.

It had been easy to accept it when her and Kate's lives had been threatened. It had been easy in the quiet of Gage's library or the strange emptiness of her new room. She'd been separated from the rest of the world, in a bubble where nothing else mattered.

But here, with the heavy reek of rotting food and urine pressing around her and reminding her of how it had all started, she couldn't remain detached. Lachlin had said she was going to lose her mind, that she couldn't handle this.

And she'd be damned if she proved Lachlin right.

She drew in a steadying breath and twisted her palm against the asphalt, focusing on the pain, on her body, on being solid within herself. Lachlin had been waiting for her head to explode since the moment she'd arrived at Gage's house. She could just imagine his smug expression when he realized she'd broken down. That was a pleasure he wasn't going to have.

Gage's scuffed boot toe stepped into sight beside her hand. "You all right?"

"Yep." Even if the only thing holding her together at the moment was her force of will, her clenched teeth, and her determination not to give Lachlin any satisfaction. "Just ah... just looking and feeling for signs of magic."

"It's rare for half-breeds to sense it," Lachlin said from deeper down the alley. "I doubt you can."

Asshole. "Well, maybe I can."

He laughed as if she'd just said the most ridiculous thing in the world. "Not likely."

She flipped him off, but he wasn't looking at her and missed it.

Gage crouched beside her, his shoulder brushing hers, sending a shiver of attraction over her. "It happened in that alley, didn't it? The one where you were stabbed four months ago. That was the first time your powers manifested."

The scar above her heart ached. "I'm fine."

"I know."

She stared at his boot toe, her nerves alight at how close he was. If she shifted just a fraction, their shoulders would brush again… or their thighs.

She clamped down on that thought and peeked at him from the corner of her eye. He stared at her, the depths of his dark eyes promising comfort, stillness. And more? Her hormones certainly wanted there to be more.

Boy, she was a mess. She jerked her attention to the dumpster a few feet away and something flickered.

What the hell? Now she was just seeing things… fine, now she was seeing more things to add to the strange things she'd started seeing four months ago.

"Morgan," he said, his voice soft.

"I'm fine. Let's finish up here."

"Sure." He straightened and she focused on his boots again. They hesitated for a second, as if he had more to say, but she wasn't going to look up to find out. Sure, on a better day without her desire racing through her, she would be stronger than this. But she had to live with the man, and she had no idea if she could trust him. He'd already lied to her about the Kin who wanted her dead. What else was he lying about?

Although perhaps this invitation out was a peace offering. It proved he wanted her on his team. But was that because he thought she'd be a good addition or because he was one of those Kin who wanted to use and control her?

No, giving in to her urges would just make an already complicated situation more complicated.

"Almost done here?" Gage asked, his boots heading deeper into the alley toward Lachlin.

"You can sense magic, too," Lachlin said. "You tell me."

And the axis of her new, topsy-turvy universe righted… at least for the moment.

If things kept up this way, she wasn't going to be able to stay long at Gage's house. That was a disaster waiting to happen.

But her reasons for moving in with Gage and his team hadn't changed. She still had no idea about this new order to the world with monsters and fairy tales. And she had no idea who she was, who her biological mother was—the source of her unwanted powers—or how to control her abilities. If she stayed with Gage, she'd be safe, relatively speaking, and others would be safe from her, but would she be safe from herself?

She glanced back at the dumpster, determined not to let her memories overwhelm her. The flicker happened again, behind and under it.

There was something there. A piece of metal catching the sunlight? Except the early afternoon sun didn't reach this far into the alley.

She knelt and pushed aside some waterlogged

newspapers—she was not going to think about what was on what she'd just touched. There, just under the edge of the dumpster, was a small silver box. It shimmered with a white halo, sparkling like a diamond in sunlight. About the size of her palm, the box had intricate Celtic-like symbols swirling over its visible sides into a mesmerizing infinity.

She grabbed a glove from the inside pocket of her new jacket—the old one hadn't survived the fight with the smoke demon—and picked it up. "I think I found something."

Gage jerked his head up. "Don't touch—"

Light exploded around them.

C.I. BLACK is the author of *The Dragon Spirit* series and *The Medusa Files* series.

She has always lived in a world of imagination. When she's not daydreaming, she puts her flights of fancy down on paper writing urban fantasy and paranormal romance books.

For the latest news on upcoming releases, you can sign up for her new release e-mail list at www.ciblack.com.